Samuel French Acting Edition

Meanwhile, Back on the Couch

A Comedy in Three Acts

by Jack Sharkey

SAMUELFRENCH.COM   SAMUELFRENCH.CO.UK

FOR PRODUCTION ENQUIRIES

UNITED STATES AND CANADA

Info@SamuelFrench.com

1-866-598-8449

UNITED KINGDOM AND EUROPE

Plays@SamuelFrench.co.uk

020-7255-4302

Each title is subject to availability from Samuel French, depending upon country of performance. Please be aware that *MEANWHILE, BACK ON THE COUCH* may not be licensed by Samuel French in your territory. Professional and amateur producers should contact the nearest Samuel French office or licensing partner to verify availability.

STORY OF THE PLAY

Psychiatrist VICTOR KARLEEN, in the throes of having fiancee GABRIELLE WINGATE's tastes reflect great expense, is distressed when friend and publisher PARKER DON-NELLY—who had been on the verge of publishing a financially rewarding book of Victor's clinical case his-tories—decides the public is tired of such books and would prefer torrid fiction, instead. Victor's special cha-grin is that fellow psychiatrist ROY TERRIGAN has, at present a greatly successful case-history book of his own on the market, and tends to gloat about royalties. When Victor's nurse CHARLOTTE HENNEBON announces the Saturday arrival of ALBERT BROCK—a rather un-happy patient who cannot come during regular weekday hours—Victor, who needs all the money he can get, takes him on with reluctance. But, to Victor's good fortune, Albert has a love-problem which is causing him to dream a rip-roaring sex novel in chaptered sequence—one chap-ter per night. Victor does not see the potential solution to his financial problems, but when his nurse accidentally puts the manuscript into the hands of the publisher, both believing it to be an original book by Victor, Victor sud-denly finds himself with a whopping big advance-royalty check which he erroneously imagines is for his casebook. By the time he catches onto the ethical, moral and legal snare in which he is entrapped, he's too far gone to resist his one chance to get a crack at the top of the best-seller list, win the hand of expensive Gabrielle, and show up his book- and love-rival Roy. But his conscience bothers him that he dare not *cure* Albert, who will stop dreaming of love if he ever actually finds it. The problem is, Albert finds love in the person of JINGLE JABONSKI, a girl from a neighboring apartment who meets him while on a scavenger hunt in Victor's office. Further complications arise when MRS. DOROTHEA MELNIK—a renegade patient of Roy's and also Albert's grandmother—decides to sock Roy with a lawsuit for his own casebook's revelations about her case, and comes to Victor for solace and therapy, scaring the hell out of him when he thinks what will happen if anyone ever finds out how he is stealing Albert's "privileged communications" to make a fortune. Complications thicken fast when Victor, in order to wring the last-chapter dream out of Albert, has to declare his love for Jingle, in order to keep Albert's love-life barren, thus messing up Victor's own love-life with Gabrielle, so that Victor can get the finished work to Parker, who is hysterically happy about the prospects of the book, already in unfinished form a nominee for a Pulitzer Prize and a mammoth movie-rights sale. How Victor saves his marriage-to-be, completes the book, foils Roy, pleases Parker, and stays out of the unemployment line makes up the plot of this fast-paced zany farce-comedy.

"MEANWHILE, BACK ON THE COUCH . . ." was presented at the Abbey Stage Door, Philadelphia, Pennsylvania, under the direction of Howard Pell with a cast as follows:

GABRIELLE WINGATE, *a talented interior decorator*

ROY TERRIGAN, *an affably unpleasant psychiatrist*

CHARLOTTE HENNEBON, *nurse/receptionist to Victor Karleen*

VICTOR KARLEEN, *psychiatrist and would-be novelist*

PARKER DONNELLY, *publisher and friend of Victor's*

ALBERT BROCK, *a young man with an old problem*

DOROTHEA MELNIK, *a disgruntled client of Roy's*

JINGLE JABONSKI, *Victor's next door neighbor*

TIME: the present

LOCALE: Victor's office/residence on Park Avenue, Manhattan

ACT ONE

A sunny Saturday morning in October

ACT TWO

The following Wednesday afternoon

ACT THREE

That evening

To my wonderful wife, Pat,
who manages to keep on
loving me while I'm
upstairs typing till
all hours of the night.

Meanwhile Back on the Couch...

ACT ONE

Curtain rises on the Manhattan office/apartment of prominent psychiatrist VICTOR KARLEEN, *on a sunny Saturday morning in October. Set is raked and jogged into three basic segments of a long single room, the right-angled corner of each segment being the farthest upstage point. From Stage Left, there is a low filing cabinet, a tall built-in bookcase containing mostly medical books but some fiction, and a tall sash-window through which we can see only the sky; the window is flanked by long draw-drapes; angling downstage from this point, there is a short staircase with railing leading to a low railed balcony, about three feet high, from which an upstage door leads to* VICTOR'S *living quarters; directly below the balcony is* VICTOR'S *desk, on which are a telephone, a notepad and a cylindrical cannister filled with pencils and pens. A swivel chair faces the desk, and the desk is flanked Left by a floorstand ashtray and Right by a rectangular wastebasket. Angling upstage from this point, we see a comfortable footstool before a matching armchair tucked into the upstage corner in which stands a tall goosenecked lamp to illuminate the chair area; angling down from the chair along the next wall segment is a leather chaise, the head-rest-section near the armchair. The final angled section has two doors at right angles to one another, with a coat tree between them in the corner; the Left door leads to a dressing room, the Right to the office anteroom or outer office; farther down along the final stretch of wall is a phonograph/liquor cabinet, beyond which stands a short rubber plant in a bright ceramic pot. The room is spacious, sunny and cheerful, and at the moment is further cheered by the presence of* GABRIELLE WINGATE, *a rather trim young lady in her early thirties, clad in sandals, pedalpushers and a man's white shirt, the front tails knotted in the front, exposing some nice bare midriff. She is on a short stepladder, downstage of the chaise and armchair, just hanging a flat-planed asymmetrical black mobile onto a hook dangling there. A paint-spattered canvas dropcloth hides the chaise, and a large abstract mural of matching paint-tones glows almost luridly on the wall just upstage of and paralleling the chaise. The door to the anteroom is slightly ajar, and a moment after curtain-rise,* DR. ROY TERRIGAN, *a fellow psychiatrist and acquaintance of* VICTOR'S, *enters and reacts pleasantly to the rear view of* GABRIELLE. ROY *is in tweeds, middle-aged, somewhat rugged of aspect, and probably smoking learnedly on a pipe. After enjoying the view a moment, he speaks.*

ROY. Nice. Very nice.
GABY. (*Reacts with mild surprise to find onlooker.*) Thank you. It *is* one of my better efforts.
ROY. What is? Oh, *that* thing! Well, that's very nice, too.
GABY. (*Gets the message, starts down ladder on:*) I seem to be distracting you—uh—?
ROY. I'm a colleague of Victor's. Roy Terrigan.
GABY. (*Folding ladder.*) I've heard Victor speak of you. I'm pleased to meet you anyway. (*He winces, but takes her extended hand with good grace, on:*) I'm Gabrielle Wingate.

Roy. *The* Gabrielle Wingate? Victor must be in the bucks! *You* charge ten dollars a minute to *look* at a wall!

Gaby. (*Gesturing from mobile to mural.*) This—is a labor of love, Dr. Terrigan. Victor and I are engaged. The decor is my wedding present to his office. (*Starts to remove dropcloth from chaise.*)

Roy. (*Catching folded ladder she has thrust his way.*) Is there a patient under there?

Gaby. No, you're next. Shave or haircut? (*Over next few lines, they will get dropcloth and ladder off into anteroom, and end up back onstage just below chaise.*)

Roy. What's a sensible girl like you doing in a psychiatrist's clutches?

Gaby. Love makes strange interior decorators.

Roy. Any girl who'd marry a psychiatrist should have her head examined. (*Laughs alone; then:*) Get it?

Gaby. My, you're everything Victor implied you'd be!

Roy. Ouch. What brought out your heavy artillery? I don't remember declaring war.

Gaby. Oh, dear, you're right. I'm sorry. It's just—

Roy. Where Victor's concerned, you're a bundle of paranoiac defense mechanisms!

Gaby. Don't psychiatrists ever go off duty?

Roy. Professional reflexes. When was the last time *you* didn't react to an unfortunate *color*-scheme?

Gaby. You're right. And I apologize. Say, would you like a drink while you're waiting for Victor?

Roy. Matter of fact, I *can't* wait for Victor. I've got an appointment with my publisher, downstairs in my apartment, in a few minutes. Tell him I'll drop by later, will you Miss Wingate?

Gaby. My friends call me "Gaby."

Roy. (*Takes her hand briefly.*) "Gaby" it is, then! (*As he backs toward anteroom door,* Victor's *nurse/ receptionist* Charlotte Hennebon *comes in, in overcoat and unbecoming hat. She is somewhat no-nonsense in demeanor, but it is only a hard-candy crust over a heart of solid marshmallow.* Charlotte *is about fifty years old, a spinster, and getting used to it.*) Oh, hi, Charlotte. Sorry I can't stop and chat.

CHARLOTTE. I'm not. I can't afford your rates. (*Exits into dressing room.*)

ROY. Who *can?* (*Exits through anteroom door. Alone,* GABY *takes stock of her workmanship, seems satisfied, then moves up to balcony door and raps lightly.*)

GABY. (*Calling through door.*) For better or worse, it's finished. Close your eyes and come on out!

(*The door opens and* VICTOR KARLEEN *comes out, eyes closed, groping a bit until* GABY *takes his outstretched hands; he is about the same age as* ROY *but nowhere near as rugged, though perhaps a bit taller. If he has any prime characteristic, it is a tendency to be overly intense about whatever he is involved in, so that any interruption or interference triggers a short-fuse temper; when it is triggered, however, the result is closer to a petulant tantrum than out-and-out rage.*)

VICTOR. Isn't this a bit childish?

GABY. (*Leading him downstairs to vantage point just below desk.*) If you really love me, you're going to have to indulge me.

VICTOR. Who was that man I heard?

GABY. (*Positioning him so that he will see all of both mobile and mural when he opens his eyes.*) Roy Terrigan. He'll be back later.

VICTOR. Thanks for the warning.

GABY. (*Surveys her work, then nods, satisfied, and:*) Okay, open up!

VICTOR. (*Looks, then stares.*) Wow! Is that thing *alive?*

GABY. The mobile or the mural?

VICTOR. Either one. They're hideously attractive!

GABY. Be careful, you may be revealing subconscious secrets. I based them on your Rorschach inkblots.

VICTOR. I'll keep my mouth shut. (*Turns to her, takes her hands.*) Gaby—the place is absolutely beautiful.

GABY. In that case, let *me* keep your mouth shut. (*Kisses him, but good; he kisses back no less ardently; while they are thus preoccupied, CHARLOTTE—now in starched white uniform and cap—enters from dressing room, comes up behind them, clears throat.*)

VICTOR. (*Breaks from clinch, sees her.*) Miss Hennebon, what are you doing here on Saturday?

CHARLOTTE. You have an appointment, Doctor Karleen.

VICTOR. But I'm taking Miss Wingate to lunch at the Plaza.

GABY. Victor, it's all right. If you have to see a patient—

VICTOR. Not on Saturday. I never see patients on Saturday.

CHARLOTTE. Albert Brock?

VICTOR. Albert—? Oh, no, is this *that* Saturday?

CHARLOTTE. And he's due here in ten minutes.

VICTOR. But I can't possibly—!

GABY. Victor, it's all right, I have to go home and change, anyway.

VICTOR. I don't deserve you.

GABY. Probably not, but you're stuck with me. (*Pecks him on the lips.*) Now, see your Mister Brock, and then I'll see you in an hour. 'Bye, Charlotte! (*With wave at nurse, exits through anteroom.*)

VICTOR. Today, of all days—!

CHARLOTTE. Saturday is the only day Mister Brock can be here.

VICTOR. Oh, it's not just lunch. Parker Donnelly is coming, too. It's hard to concentrate on Mister Brock's problems when I'm totally tangled in my own!

CHARLOTTE. How *is* your book coming along, Doctor? Does Mister Donnelly like it?

VICTOR. He's supposed to let me know today,

CHARLOTTE. I'm sure it will be all right, Doctor. I mean, he's not just your publisher, he's your friend.
VICTOR. That's true. So why am I so jumpy?
CHARLOTTE. Maybe your shorts are too tight.
PARKER. (*Off.*) Victor?
VICTOR. (*Galvanized.*) It's him!
CHARLOTTE. (*Starting toward anteroom.*) I'll go scrub a syringe or something.

(PARKER DONNELLY *enters before she is quite off; he is the tall, suave, dapper, British-tailor-and-homburg-hat type, with trim sideburns and moustache; he carries a typewritten manuscript.*)

PARKER. Ah, there you are, Victor! And how are *you*, Nurse Hennebon?
CHARLOTTE. Still single. (*Exits to anteroom, shuts door.*)
VICTOR. Well . . . ?
PARKER. (*Uncomfortably.*) Well . . .
VICTOR. (*Sinks to sit on edge of chaise.*) You *did* read my book?
PARKER. Yes, indeed. A sterling job. Some really amazing case histories. One of the most colorful psychiatric casebooks I've ever read. I loved it. Really.
VICTOR. Then why aren't we dancing around the room?
PARKER. Welllllll. . . .
VICTOR. That word again! (*Jumps up.*) I'm going to have a drink! (*Heads for cabinet.*) Will you join me? I hate to drink alone. No, that's not true. I *love* to drink alone.
PARKER. Bourbon on the rocks is fine.
VICTOR. (*At cabinet, fixing two stiff drinks.*) Now, Park, I don't want friendship to interfere with your professional judgment. If you didn't like the book, don't give me empty encouragement. No, wait—maybe a *little* empty encouragement . . .
PARKER. (*Sets manuscript on desk, sits on lower right

corner of desk, choosing his words carefully.) You know I wouldn't do that, Vic. The book is good. Extremely good—of its kind.

VICTOR. (*Still fixing drinks.*) But you still haven't asked me to dance.

PARKER. Do you realize we've published a dozen such books over the past ten years?

VICTOR. (*Bringing drinks across room.*) *Yes,* I know how many you've published! And the latest one is the work of Doctor Roy Terrigan! All he talks is royalty statements! Sometimes, I think I wrote my book just to be "one up" on Roy! Well, whyever I did it . . . (*Hands drink to* PARKER.) *My* book's a hell of a lot better than *his!* (*Drains half his drink.*) Even his *title* stinks! (*Quotes:*) "IT'S ALL IN THE MIND"! Yucchh!

PARKER. (*Quietly.*) Victor—*I* made up the title for Roy's book . . .

VICTOR. (*Staggered, but fast on his feet.*) See? His book was so rotten that even *you* had to admit it! (*Ever the psychiatrist.*) Subconsciously, you *knew* it stank, so your professionalism forced you to conjure up a stinky *name* for it!

PARKER. (*Enough of a friend to drop the topic.*) Be that as it may, Vic—I'm afraid we won't be publishing your book this season.

VICTOR. But it's good . . .

PARKER. And we've done a dozen in ten years. The market is glutted. The public is looking for something else. Its prospects are limited. (*Beat.*) And the board of directors overruled my recommendation.

VICTOR. (*Raises his glass.*) Well—for that I thank you. There goes a year-and-a-half of typing my fingers to the bone—and a Caribbean honeymoon. (*Tosses off remainder of drink.*)

PARKER. I didn't follow that part about the honeymoon.

VICTOR. (*Gestures at room.*) This charming little apartment/office combination has set back the Karleen exchequer a big bundle, buddy. You want Park Avenue, you pay for Park Avenue. Then there's the cumulative cost of wining and dining and wooing Gaby—a girl you don't take to the nearest Nedick's for a cream-cheese-and-olive sandwich. Not to mention all those psycho-analyze-yourself articles in Readers Digest that keep the patients away in droves. Do you think I'd be seeing Albert Brock on a Saturday if I didn't need the dough?

PARKER. What's his problem?

VICTOR. The same problem *everybody* has!

PARKER. Boy meets girl, boy doesn't get girl?

VICTOR. I forgot you read psychiatric casebooks. The older I get, the more I think that's the *only* problem there is—not getting loved back.

PARKER. Well, at least *you* don't have that problem.

VICTOR. But just wait'll I ask Gaby to swap a Caribbean cruise for a ride on the Staten Island Ferry!

PARKER. I can stake you to a weekend on Bear Mountain . . .

VICTOR. Don't laugh, I may take you up on it! (*Holds up empty glass.*) Another one?

PARKER. (*Shakes head, stands.*) No, I still have a few ports of call before I meet my wife for dinner and the theater. (*Carries own glass to cabinet, on:*) But if you write anything else I can peddle for you, give me a ring.

VICTOR. Such *as?*

PARKER. What we were just talking about: Sex.

VICTOR. *Were* we?

PARKER. What do you think boy-meets-girl is, the basis for a discussion group? It's sex, boy, sex!

VICTOR. But I don't know a thing about it!

PARKER. In that case, not even Bear Mountain will help!

VICTOR. I don't mean *sex*, you clown, I mean writing a novel about it!

PARKER. (*At door to anteroom.*) If you *did* write one, and it sold like sex novels usually sell—Dr. Roy Terrigan's casebook of psychiatry would look mighty sick by comparison. He's sold forty thousand copies—you could quadruple that.

VICTOR. What makes you think *I*—?

PARKER. I've read your case book. If you could put your patients' hangups into a racy novel—*zowie!*

VICTOR. But, *I* can't write! I don't know a *thing* about *plotting . . . !*

PARKER. It was just an idea. (*Opens door.*) Thanks for the drink, Vic. And I'm sorry. (*Exits.*)

VICTOR. (*Aloud, to himself.*) *He's* sorry! (*Starts making himself new drink.*) Miss Hennebon—! Have we discussed my fee with Albert Brock?

CHARLOTTE. (*Leans in anteroom door for:*) We *haggled* over it. He's paying the minimum rate—twenty-five dollars an hour.

VICTOR. Book him solid for the next hundred hours!

CHARLOTTE. When will you sleep?

VICTOR. While he's talking. Very few patients peep over the back of the couch.

CHARLOTTE. What about your snoring?

VICTOR. Who told you I snore?

CHARLOTTE. Your other patients. (*Exits.*)

VICTOR. (*Takes vicious sip of drink.*) This is going to be a hell of a day—first "The Continuing Story of Roy and His Royalties"—now the latest episode of "Chuckles the Nurse"! (*Strides to desk, lifts manuscript, then sighs, drops it, and takes another sip.*) Forty thousand copies! And he never stops talking about them!

CHARLOTTE. (*Enters on:*) Mister Brock is here, Doctor Karleen.

VICTOR. Did he bring his wallet?

CHARLOTTE. I'll frisk him and see.

VICTOR. Oh, send him in, send him in!

(CHARLOTTE *exits,* VICTOR *sees he is still holding drink, bolts across room to put it inside cabinet, starts away, then grabs it up and drains it, puts the empty glass back, and runs to his desk, where he has just taken a leisurely left-hand-in-jacket-pocket-and-right-hand-flat-on-desk stance facing the door when* ALBERT BROCK *edges timidly in.* ALBERT *is short, wearing neat but ill-fitted clothing, and could be anywhere from twenty to fifty-five years of age—he probably had this frazzled look and appearance at age fifteen, and will still have it at seventy-five.*)

ALBERT. The nurse said I should come in.

VICTOR. (*Professionally charming, now.*) And so you should, Albert. Here, sit down on the couch and relax. This isn't going to hurt. (*As* ALBERT *sits,* VICTOR *gets notepad and pencil, moves to armchair.*)

ALBERT. It's sure nice of you to see me on a Saturday, Doctor.

VICTOR. Don't think of me as your doctor; think of me as your friend. (*Sits in armchair, turns on lamp, opens pad and gets pencil ready to take notes.*) Now please lie back, relax, and tell me anything that may be troubling you.

ALBERT. (*Lies back; then:*) This is going to wrinkle my suit.

VICTOR. Really, Albert—!

ALBERT. You said "anything"—

VICTOR. Yes. Yes, I did. All right, Albert. I admit, it may wrinkle your suit, but we're going to smooth out your complexes.

ALBERT. It cost forty dollars.

VICTOR. (*Chokes off a curt retort; says calmly:*) It is your mind we must concern ourselves with. Relax, put your trust in me, and tell me your troubles.

ALBERT. Well, it's these continuing *dreams* of mine . . .

VICTOR. Would you care to tell me about them?

ALBERT. All of them?

VICTOR. If you like.

ALBERT. (*Fumbles inside jacket.*) I wrote down the first nine. Let me show you . . . . (*Pulls bundle of folded sheets of paper from inner pocket.*)

VICTOR. That was good thinking, Albert. Did you write them down the moment you awakened?

ALBERT. Yes, so I wouldn't forget them.

VICTOR. I admire your foresight, Albert— (*Takes papers which* ALBERT, *without looking back, passes overhead to him.*) Not many men would think of writing the dreams down before they could be forgotten.

ALBERT. Oh, I didn't.

VICTOR. Didn't write them down?

ALBERT. Didn't think of it. I got the idea from an article in Readers Digest.

VICTOR. (*Wearily.*) Where else! (*Leans forward and drops papers onto footstool, leans back and gets ready to take notes again.*) But tell me, Albert—when did these bothersome dreams begin?

ALBERT. Ten nights ago. Right after I found my grandmother's picture.

VICTOR. Ah! You were close to your grandmother, were you?

ALBERT. No, she was in the basement, tending the furnace. Of course, it's not very far, as the crow flies.

VICTOR. Your grandmother is still living?

ALBERT. Boy, is she ever! She's one of my boarders. Never misses a meal.

VICTOR. (*Pinches the bridge of his nose; he is beginning to get a headache.*) My—my memory seems to be shortchanging me, today, Albert— Just exactly *what* is it you do, again?

ALBERT. I run a boarding house in Brooklyn. Up at six, fix breakfast, call the boarders, serve the food, do the dishes, bring in the mail, put it in the proper rooms, vacuum the parlor, clean the rooms, grab a bite of lunch, do the marketing, come home, put the food away, start dinner, clean the dining room—

VICTOR. Uh— Albert—

ALBERT. —set the table, serve the dinner, do the dishes, clean the dining room again—

VICTOR. Albert—

ALBERT. —say goodnight to everyone, lock up the doors and windows, and go to bed.

VICTOR. (*On the scent, pencil poised.*) And that's when you have these dreams?

ALBERT. Only since I found my grandmother's picture.

VICTOR. Now, wait—backtrack a bit—what does this picture mean to you?

ALBERT. Nothing. But it means an awful lot to my grandmother.

VICTOR. And it's important to keep your grandmother happy?

ALBERT. Oh, yes, very important!

VICTOR. (*On the scent again.*) What exactly is your relationship with your grandmother?

ALBERT. I'm her grandson.

VICTOR. *I know that!* (*Pinches bridge of nose again.*) I'm sorry. I didn't mean to shout.

ALBERT. Then why did you?

VICTOR. (*Controlling himself.*) Look—it's this way, Albert— I am trying to delve into your unconscious motivations—and you are climbing your family tree! I want to know why finding your grandmother's picture was so meaningful to you.

ALBERT. Because it made my grandmother happy.

VICTOR. Ah! And why is your grandmother's happiness of such importance?

ALBERT. I need the rent. Her room costs twenty-five dollars a week.

VICTOR. Look—no, wait—we'll try another approach. You say your dreams seem to stem from the time you found her picture. Why do you say that?

ALBERT. Because it's true.

VICTOR. Okay. Okay. Granted, it's true. But when you looked at this picture, and saw your grandmother—

ALBERT. Oh, it's not a picture of my grandmother.

VICTOR. But you said—

ALBERT. It's my grandmother's picture. But it's a picture of Charlton Heston.

VICTOR. *Charlton Heston?!*

ALBERT. Autographed. "To Annabel, with many thanks."

VICTOR. Ah, your grandmother's name is Annabel!

ALBERT. No.

VICTOR. But—if it's her picture—

ALBERT. She got it from Annabel. For a Gary Cooper and a George Raft.

VICTOR. Albert—

ALBERT. But Annabel wanted to get Charlton Heston back, because the George Raft picture was all scruffy on the back, and she couldn't read all the words.

VICTOR. What words?

ALBERT. When he was born, what movies he'd been in —like that.

VICTOR. Albert—this picture—it sounds like a bubble-gum card.

ALBERT. It is. That's what made the back all scruffy. My grandmother has sweaty hands, and the bubble gum got kind of soft, and—

VICTOR. *Hold it! (Covers eyes with one hand for a second; then:)* Maybe—maybe you'd better just tell me your dream . . .

ALBERT. Annabel can't chew bubble-gum anyhow, because of her dentures. That's why my grandmother peeled off the gum before she traded.

VICTOR. The dream, Albert, the dream!

ALBERT. Oh. Okay. Well, like I said, I was looking at the picture, and it reminded me of when I went to the movies with my grandmother.

VICTOR. A childhood memory! Good! Tell me about it.

ALBERT. Well, not exactly childhood. We only started last August.

VICTOR. Never in your childhood?

ALBERT. No. My grandmother didn't need glasses, then.

VICTOR. But now she does? So now you go?

ALBERT. Well, you see, she can't see the screen very

well, so I have to describe the movies to her. I mean, she can hear what the people are saying, all right, but I tell her to ignore that.

VICTOR. Why do you tell her to ignore what the people are saying?

ALBERT. Well, I mean, if I want to describe the movie to my grandmother who can't see the screen, why not?

VICTOR. Why not *what?!*

ALBERT. Ignore them. Wouldn't you?

VICTOR. But how does your grandmother know what the movie is about, if she doesn't listen to the actors?

ALBERT. Oh, she *tries* to listen to the actors, in between my descriptions of the scenes, but how can she, with all the people saying, "Hey, quiet down there!"

VICTOR. You mean the people in the audience!? *That's* who you tell her to ignore?!

ALBERT. Who did you think I meant?

VICTOR. (*Covers eyes again for a second; then:*) I believe I'm getting a headache.

ALBERT. Do you still want to hear my dream?

VICTOR. Is your grandmother in it?

ALBERT. No.

VICTOR. Then I'd love to!

ALBERT. Where was I?

VICTOR. Your grandmother misplaced her picture of Charlton Heston, you found it and gave it back so she'd be happy and pay her rent, but the picture reminded you of the movies, and that night you had your first dream.

ALBERT. You make it sound to simple!

VICTOR. *One* of us has to!

ALBERT. Do you want to know who Annabel is?

VICTOR. Strangely enough, no.

ALBERT. She's another one of my boarders.

VICTOR. Excuse me a moment, Albert . . . (*Rises and crosses to phonograph, on:*) Sometimes, in recounting a dream, a little harmonious mood music is of vast assistance . . . (*Unseen by* ALBERT, *he will pour and drink a good stiff bourbon without benefit of rocks, on:*)

ALBERT. Do you have anything with violins? There wasn't any mood music in the dream, but I think violins would go good with it . . .

VICTOR. (*Putting on a record.*) I think maybe a bit of Brahms should suit the situation. Let me just adjust the volume . . . there! (*The soft strains of "Brahms Lullaby"—the best-known of the dozen-or-so he wrote—come from the phonograph, as* VICTOR *returns to his chair and pad and pencil, during:*) Now, I just want you to lie back, relax, and tell me your dream—leaving out no detail, no matter how insignificant it may seem.

ALBERT. (*As* VICTOR *sits down.*) Well, first—I want to make sure of something . . .

VICTOR. (*He's heard this one before.*) Now, now, have no fears about my discretion, Albert. The dialogue between psychiatrist and patient is sacred. My lips are sealed like a priest in the confessional.

ALBERT. The priest is sealed in the confessional?

VICTOR. His *lips* are!

ALBERT. What's the penalty for telling?

VICTOR. Albert, I have no intention of telling—

ALBERT. But what if you do? I mean, if a priest blabs he goes to hell. What happens if a psychiatrist blabs? Where does *he* go?

VICTOR. On welfare!

ALBERT. Going to hell sounds worse than going on welfare.

VICTOR. Have you ever *been* on welfare?

ALBERT. No. Knock on wood. (*Tries knocking on chaise with poor results.*)

VICTOR. Then take my word for it!

ALBERT. But—hell is sure-fire—the psychiatrist may not go *anyplace!*

VICTOR. (*Despite himself.*) At this rate, not even Bear Mountain! (*"Brahms Lullaby" can end any time from here on, and phonograph shut off.*)

ALBERT. (*Half-rises.*) Hmm?

VICTOR. (*Recovers.*) A professional joke. Forget it. Lie back down, please. (ALBERT *does; then:*) Now, if you'll just tell me last night's dream . . . ?

ALBERT. Why are dreams so important to psychiatrists?

VICTOR. (*With frayed patience:*) Because they are *symbols*—signposts to the subconscious. When a man dreams, he *disguises* his real troubles from himself. It is the task of the psychiatrist to find what they mean, and show the patient what his *real* problem is.

ALBERT. I don't understand.

VICTOR. (*Wearily sets pad on lap, downs pencil, and prepares for a mini-lecture.*) It's like this, Albert. Symbols vary from person to person. What means one thing to one man may mean something different to another. Do you follow me so far?

ALBERT. I *think* so . . . ?

VICTOR. Okay, let's say a man dreams he is locked inside a steel box. Now, he is not *really* afraid he is going to be locked inside a steel box. That box *represents something*—trapped in a job he hates—locked up in a marriage he cannot tolerate—being deeply in debt— But his subconscious doesn't come right out and say it—

ALBERT. Why not?

VICTOR. Don't ask *me! I* didn't invent the subconscious mind! It just *does*, and that's all there is *to* it!

ALBERT. Gee, that's fascinating! I've been wondering a lot about some of the things in my dreams. Now I understand that they don't really mean what they seem to. What *do* they mean?

VICTOR. I can hardly hazard a guess until you *tell* me some of them!

ALBERT. Oh, sure. That makes sense.

VICTOR. I'm glad *one* of us is making some sense! No. Wait. I'm sorry.

ALBERT. (*With genuine amicability.*) Oh, that's okay. I know I drive people crazy. That's one of my big problems. Instant aggravation.

VICTOR. (*Contrite.*) That's all right, go ahead, Albert, relax. I'd like to hear some of your dream symbols, really.

ALBERT. Okay . . . (*Thinks a second; then:*) What does it mean when you dream you're alone with a gorgeous girl, and you grab her in your arms, and you kiss her and kiss her, and hold her tight, and kiss her some more?

VICTOR. (*Stymied.*) Uh—what do *you* think it means . . . ?

ALBERT. Well—I *did* think it meant I was crazy for girls, but since you told me about this symbolism-stuff, I realize it must mean something else entirely, right?

VICTOR. (*Caught in his own pedantry.*) Well—you see —um—there are *some* things, Albert—I mean—the subconscious doesn't *always* use symbols—sometimes the message shouts out loud and clear . . .

ALBERT. You mean that other guy—the one you told me about—might *really* be afraid of getting locked in a steel box?

VICTOR. (*Loses control.*) Well, who *wouldn't* be?!

ALBERT. But the symbolism—?

VICTOR. (*Gets a grip on himself.*) Look, let's make this session easy on both of us. Why don't you just tell me your dream, and I'll be the judge of what's a symbol and what isn't, okay?

ALBERT. Well, gee, *sure*, Doctor! Whatever you say. What do you want me to do?

VICTOR. Lie back. Close your eyes. Breathe deeply and slowly . . . (ALBERT *has done each in turn; then:*) Now, as clearly as you can recall—what was your dream? (ALBERT *lies silent one beat, then gently begins to snore.*) Albert? . . . Albert—? . . . *ALBERT!!!*

ALBERT. (*Bounds up from chaise, terrified.*) What is it? What happened? Where am I?

VICTOR. I thought you'd prefer doing Dream Number Eleven in your *free* time.

ALBERT. Oh gee, thanks. (*Sits on edge of chaise.*) It's just, my job leaves me so tired . . . (*Will recline slowly, during:*) Monday through Friday—six a.m. to nine p.m. —and three o'clock to nine p.m. on Saturdays and Sundays . . .

VICTOR. Those *are* back-breaking hours! Why do you do it?

ALBERT. Money. You don't know what it means to always be needing money.

VICTOR. (*Almost argues the point, but stops himself.*) Oh . . . I can *imagine* what it's like.

ALBERT. It's such a monotonous life, too. If I hadn't inherited the boarding house, I'd never pick it as a life's work.

VICTOR. Who did you inherit it from?

ALBERT. My grandmother.

VICTOR. But—she isn't *dead* yet!

ALBERT. She said if she hadn't given me the boarding house, she *would* have been.

VICTOR. She *gave* you the boarding house? For free?

ALBERT. Well, not exactly. I kind of *lease* it from her for forty dollars a week.

VICTOR. But *her* rent is only twenty-five! She comes out fifteen dollars ahead!

ALBERT. Well, she dates a lot.

VICTOR. How old is your grandmother, Albert?

ALBERT. Seventy-five. But you'd never know it when she's all dolled up.

VICTOR. Albert—these hours of yours—can't you get some *help* running the boarding house?

ALBERT. Oh, I've *asked* my grandmother, but she's always got a date.

VICTOR. Well, look—have you ever considered getting married?

ALBERT. I never consider anything else! Someone young . . . tender . . . strong . . .

VICTOR. Then why not *do* something about it? Find a girl—take her out—fall in love—!

ALBERT. Find her *where?* Take her out with *what?* Fall in love *when?*

VICTOR. (*Considers this, then bends over pad with pencil again, and:*) Tell me your dream, Albert . . . (*PHONE rings.*) Oh, excuse me— (*Half-rises.*)

ALBERT. (*Sits up.*) You're going to *answer* that—? On *my* twenty-five dollars?

VICTOR. (*Stymied.*) Well—uh— (*PHONE starts to ring again, cuts off in mid-ring.*) Oh, I guess Miss Hennebon got it. (*Settles back into armchair.*) Go ahead, Albert.

ALBERT. (*Settling back onto chaise, still a bit miffed.*) After all, what's a receptionist for?

VICTOR. It's all right, Albert. Go on with your dream.

ALBERT. I mean, it's *my* hour I'm paying for, and if the phone rings—

VICTOR. *Tell me the damned dream!* (*Hand over eyes again.*) Sorry. I shouldn't shout.

ALBERT. I understand. You're very tense, aren't you?!

VICTOR. More than ever, lately. It's this man—this other psychiatrist—he keeps needling me, day in, day out—

ALBERT. Of course. And you have to lash out at somebody, so when a patient comes in—

VICTOR. You're very understanding, Albert. Sometimes, I could just sit right down and cry, I'm so— (*Realizes:*) Wait a minute! *Who's* analyzing *who,* for pete's sake?!

ALBERT. I was only trying to help.

VICTOR. Just . . . tell me your dream, Albert . . . that would be a *big* help.

ALBERT. All right. I—I hardly know how to begin . . .

VICTOR. (*Pad and pencil ready, speaks soothingly.*) Now, now, just relax, and begin at the beginning . . .

(*Over next speech,* VICTOR *will at first take his notes methodically, nodding his head in indication that he is following; then he will slowly raise his head and stare straight out front, as it dawns on him that this is not quite par-for-the-course dream-recounting;*

finally, he will turn his head and stare unbelievingly at ALBERT, *just before his own interruptive speech.*)

ALBERT. Okay, here goes: "She lay there on the green velvet sofa, staring up into his face. 'No, Sidney!' she breathed. 'We mustn't! It's—it's *wrong*, Sidney!' But then his mouth was crushing hers, his arms encircling her writhing body, till suddenly she felt her own arms move of their own volition about his neck. The room seemed to shimmer—to spin—to turn a soft molten red and sag into a crimson abyss of caressing fires, and—"

VICTOR. Albert—?

ALBERT. Yes, Doctor?

VICTOR. What the hell are you telling me?

ALBERT. My dream. Number Ten.

VICTOR. But—who *is* this woman? Who is Sidney? What are these people to you?

ALBERT. (*Sits up, speaks matter-of-factly.*) Well, the woman is Jessica Lathrop. She's married to Sir Frederick Lathrop—a man she adores—but he's off on business for a month, and his valet, Sidney, who knows Jessica is hideously lonely—

VICTOR. Wait a minute, wait a minute! How do you know all this?

ALBERT. Oh, it was all made quite clear in Dream Number Nine.

VICTOR. You mean you're dreaming about these people in *sequence?*

ALBERT. Yeah. Ten dreams in a row. The story continues from night to night. It's called—

VICTOR. Your dream has a *title?*

ALBERT. Sure. Why not?

VICTOR. Because—well—a dream is just a—I mean—it has a *title?*

ALBERT. A title, and a setting, and minor characters, and a sub-plot—and—

VICTOR. But Albert—that's *crazy!*

ALBERT. Why do you think I'm *here?!* (*While* VICTOR *thinks this over, there is a RAP at the door.*)

VICTOR. (*Looks at wristwatch.*) That must be Miss Hennebon. I'm afraid your hour is up, Albert. (*Turns off lamp.*)

ALBERT. But I haven't finished my dream—

VICTOR. Well, look, I tell you what— (*RAP again.*) Just a minute, Albert— (*Calls.*) Come in! (*As* CHARLOTTE *enters, he continues.*) Why don't you write *this* dream down, too, and—

ALBERT. Oh, I did. (*Fumbles some papers out of pocket during:*) I just thought you'd want to hear it first-hand, so you could comment on it as I went along . . .

VICTOR. (*A bit dazed, takes papers.*) That—that was very foresighted of you, Albert . . . (*Sees* CHARLOTTE *hovering at door.*) I'm sorry, Miss Hennebon— What is it?

CHARLOTTE. There's a Mrs. Melnik on the line. She wants an appointment.

VICTOR. I don't know any Mrs. Melnik. Who recommended her?

CHARLOTTE. She didn't say. But she's good for the full fifty dollars an hour.

VICTOR. I'll take her.

ALBERT. (*Before* CHARLOTTE *can turn to go.*) Is that Mrs. *Dorothea* Melnik?

CHARLOTTE. Why, yes it is. Do *you* know her, Mister Brock?

ALBERT. She's one of my boarders.

VICTOR. Ah, then *you* recommended me to her, is that it?

ALBERT. No. *She* recommended you to *me.*

CHARLOTTE. I don't follow you.

VICTOR. (*Covers eyes as before.*) Welcome to the club.

ALBERT. (*It hasn't fazed him.*) Well, I've got to get back to Brooklyn. (*Takes step toward door.*)

CHARLOTTE. And you're *hurrying?*

ALBERT. I have a roast in the oven. (*To* VICTOR.) Next Saturday, same time, all right with you?

VICTOR. (*Spreads hands, shrugs.*) Why not! (*Before* ALBERT *can exit*, ROY *enters.*)

ROY. Victor, do you know a Mrs. Dorothea Melnik?!

VICTOR. No, but apparently I'm the only one who doesn't!

CHARLOTTE. Oh, my, I've left that poor woman waiting on the phone! Doctor, is next Wednesday all right?

ALBERT. (*Exits to anteroom on:*) I'll *ask* her . . .

VICTOR. (*Shouts after him:*) She meant is it all right with *me!*

ALBERT. (*Off.*) Well, is it?

VICTOR. Yes, yes! It's just fine!

ROY. Well, it's not fine with *me!*

VICTOR. (*Lurches toward liquor cabinet, where he will fix a fresh drink for himself.*) What do you care *when* I see my patient?

ROY. But that's just it—she's *not* your patient, she's *my* patient!

CHARLOTTE. You mean she *was!*

ROY. I mean she *is!* And she certainly can't see *both* of us!

CHARLOTTE. Maybe she's got a split personality. (*Exits to anteroom.*)

ROY. Victor, how do you *stand* that woman?

VICTOR. She works cheap. (*Takes satisfying sip of drink.*) But honestly, Roy, until this Melnik woman phoned, I had never even *heard* of her. If she wants to switch over to me—

ROY. Where are your ethics? You can't hijack another analyst's patient from under his nose and—

(GABY *enters from anteroom, smartly dressed as befits an upcoming trip to the Plaza—probably a well-cut suit, chic hat and fur stole.*)

GABY. Ready for lunch, darling? . . . Oh, hello, Roy.

Roy. Gaby—! I'm glad you're here. Maybe *you* can talk some ethics into this unprincipled practitioner! Do you know you're engaged to a *bodysnatcher?*

Gaby. Mmm, *do* I! (Victor *laughs.*)

Roy. Oh, well done, well done! You two are just *made* for each other!

Gaby. Are you men having a squabble?

Victor. (*Has just drained drink, sets glass on cabinet.*) *He* is having a squabble, darling. *I* am having lunch with the sweetest woman in the western world.

Charlotte. (*Enters on:*) I've already *had* my lunch. (*As* Victor *covers his eyes again:*) I told Mrs. Melnik Wednesday will be fine and dandy.

Roy. Well, *I* intend to pray for *rain!* (*Stalks out through anteroom; then we hear outer door SLAM.*)

Gaby. Victor, darling, what *was* that all about?

Victor. A patient of Roy's has decided to become a patient of mine.

Charlotte. During one of her lucid moments.

Victor. (*Starts toward desk.*) Well, if you'll bear with me, darling, it's *my* turn to go and change for lunch. Why don't you have a drink while you wait? (*Puts Dream Number Ten with other nine dreams on desktop, hefts his book manuscript, then ruefully drops it into desk drawer, during:*)

Charlotte. Don't mind if I do. (*Starts for cabinet.*)

Gaby. (*Moving more slowly after her.*) How many should I have, Victor? I mean, to catch up to you?

Victor. (*Heading for stairs.*) You can't possibly catch up to me. I started before you were born.

Charlotte. (*Fixing two drinks.*) *Long* before you were born!

Victor. (*Pauses at balcony door for:*) If I *wanted* amplification I would have *asked* for amplification. (*Starts into living quarters, then pauses for:*) Oh, Miss Hennebon—if you get the chance—could you possibly retype those pages on my desk? The handwriting is nearly illegible.

CHARLOTTE. Well, I *was* going out on the town with the Count of Monte Cristo, tonight, but he's too hard (*Hands one of two drinks to* GABY.) to get out of the sack! (VICTOR *whinnies through gritted teeth, exits from balcony, shuts door.*)

GABY. (*Laughing.*) Charlotte, you're incorrigible. (*Sees* VICTOR *is gone, turns confidential.*) Listen—before he comes back—what *was* that squabble all about? Victor's been so edgy these past few weeks. I thought it was just a good case of premarital nerves—but lately I'm not so sure . . .

CHARLOTTE. I think it's his book, Miss Wingate. He's very concerned about it hitting the best seller list. What with Doctor Terrigan's book selling so well . . .

GABY. How *is* Roy's book doing?

CHARLOTTE. Not bad. It nosed its way into the Top Ten one week, but then it slid right out again. So Doctor Karleen doesn't just want to edge *into* the Top Ten— he wants a crack at the Number One spot.

GABY. (*Sits on chaise, sips thoughtfully at drink; then:*) Do you think Victor's book has a chance?

CHARLOTTE. Mister Donnelly seems to think so. It's amazing the things a nurse can hear through a closed door—with a stethoscope.

GABY. Charlotte!

CHARLOTTE. Are you shocked?

GABY. Scandalized. What did he say about the book?

CHARLOTTE. Something about its sales quadrupling Doctor Terrigan's, if Doctor Karleen can work a *plot* into it. I got the impression that sex is where it's at for the big money.

GABY. But Victor wouldn't— (*Stops and looks toward papers on desk.*) Or would he? (*Stands, still looking.*) You don't suppose—?

CHARLOTTE. (*Races* GABY *to desk.*) If Doctor Karleen is writing about sex, it would explain why the handwriting is illegible! His hands shake when *I* come near him! (GABY *grabs up papers first.*) Is there anything in there that a thirty-year-old nurse shouldn't see?

GABY. (*Starting to read, reacts and looks up.*) Thirty?

CHARLOTTE. I wasn't asking for myself.

GABY. (*Looks at papers again, then her eyebrows rise.*) I'm not sure I should even tell you the *title!*

CHARLOTTE. I have to *type* the damned thing, don't I? (*Squirms into position for a peek at top sheet.*) Holy Toledo! Am I reading that right?

GABY. What does it look like to you?

CHARLOTTE. *"Meanwhile, Back at the Wench . . . !"*

GABY. That's what I *thought* it said! I didn't know Victor had it in him!

CHARLOTTE. (*Takes papers, sets her drink on desk.*) Still waters run deep. (*Looks at first page.*) But these waters are *galloping!*

GABY. Listen, I'm not sure Victor wants me sneaking a look at his book before publication. You'd better keep these away from me. After all, if a man can't trust his own fiancee . . .

CHARLOTTE. Shall I type you a carbon copy?

GABY. Of course.

CHARLOTTE. (*Starts for dressing room door.*) I think I'll make one for my Aunt Minnie, too. She's eighty years old, and her lips have never touched anything but beer. Maybe this'll help her morale. (*Exits into dressing room. GABY takes her glass and CHARLOTTE's over to cabinet, has just set them down when VICTOR, spruced and combed and carrying his overcoat over his arm, enters on balcony.*)

VICTOR. (*Sings an introductory fanfare:*) *Ta-daaa!* Here I am, ready or not.

GABY. You mean take-it-or-leave-it, don't you? (*Crosses to meet him below chaise.*)

VICTOR. What does it take to get a kind word out of you?

GABY. Now, darling, if I was all sickening sweetness,

you'd think I didn't love you anymore. (*Takes his hands as they meet.*)

VICTOR. Stop talking and kiss me! (*She does, and he returns the favor with interest, and while they are thus preoccupied,* ALBERT—*now in topcoat—enters from anteroom.*)

GABY. (*Pulls back for air.*) How did you ever develop such terrific arm-muscles?

VICTOR. I work out with *dumbbells* every day!

GABY. (*Starts a laugh, stops as she sees* ALBERT.) Oops, we have an audience. (*She and* VICTOR *part quickly.*) We thought you'd gone home, Mister Brock.

ALBERT. I got downstairs and realized I hadn't paid my twenty-five dollars. (*Holds out fistful of bills.*)

VICTOR. (*Steps between* GABY *and* ALBERT.) You really needn't have bothered, Albert. We could have settled up next session. Money is of secondary importance— (*Unseen by* GABY, *grabs bills and jams them into suit pocket.*) Getting you well is what counts.

GABY. (*Steps between them, oblivious to the way* ALBERT *stares numbly at his empty hand, for:*) We were just leaving—can we drop you anyplace?

ALBERT. You're sure it wouldn't be too much trouble?

VICTOR. I'd like nothing better than dropping you someplace, Albert. (*Both stare at him; he covers with forced laugh.*) Crosstown subway station all right?

ALBERT. It's a step in the right direction.

GABY. (*Links her arm in* VICTOR'S.) Then it's settled. Let's go, darling. I'm absolutely famished.

VICTOR. (*Unconsciously touching money-pocket.*) Now, don't go and spoil that lovely figure before the wedding.

GABY. Oh, I never gain weight. It's glands or something. Eat, eat, eat and never put on an ounce.

ALBERT. Gee, I wish *I* had a girl like you!

VICTOR. Make me an offer. (*As both stare at him again, he forces another laugh and marshals them out through anteroom; we hear outer door SHUT, and then* CHARLOTTE, *once more in topcoat and that hat, enters from dressing room, holding* ALBERT'S *scribbled dreams; she looks about, straightens pad and pencil-container on desk, and as she starts for the anteroom door, the PHONE rings; she gets it.*)

CHARLOTTE. (*On phone:*) Doctor Karleen's office . . . Oh, I'm sorry, Doctor Terrigan, you just missed them . . . Mrs. Melnik? Yes, of *course* I remember about her . . . She's *suing* you?! For *what?* . . . (PARKER *enters from anteroom in topcoat, sees she is on phone, stands where he is.*) Well, I'm afraid we'll *have* to see her next Wednesday—she's all booked, and I don't see that it makes that much difference . . . What have *ethics* got to do with it?— Doctor Terrigan?— Hello? . . . (*Shrugs, hangs up; then, to* PARKER:) Can I help you, Mister Donnelly?

PARKER. Uh—well— Is Victor here?

CHARLOTTE. He and Miss Wingate just left. If it's important, you can catch him at the Plaza . . .

PARKER. Well, actually—it's his *book* I'm here about. You see, we—uh—there's been a sort of upset in our schedule, and—well—

CHARLOTTE. You call a defamation-of-character suit a *sort* of upset?

PARKER. Terrigan *told* you?

CHARLOTTE. He cried in my ear.

PARKER. Good. That makes it easier. You see, we were planning a new edition of his book, but since this Mrs. Melnik recognized herself in it, and instituted her lawsuit—

CHARLOTTE. You're yanking his book and you hope Doctor Karleen's can fill the gap?

PARKER. Well, a book is a book.

CHARLOTTE. Doctor Karleen will be terribly flattered.

PARKER. Confound it, Charlotte, I'm desperate! Look —the impending lawsuit forces us to get Terrigan's book right off the shelves, but the attendant *publicity* is going to make casebooks more popular than ever. And Victor's is ripe and ready. I don't care if he's flattered or not. The money will change his mind.

CHARLOTTE. You must have a very low opinion of Doctor Karleen.

PARKER. No, I have a very high opinion of money. But look—that *was* Terrigan on the phone just now—? . . . Why would he warn Victor about Mrs. Melnik's lawsuit?

CHARLOTTE. Professional courtesy. Besides—

PARKER. He hopes Victor will give her an overdose of scopolamine?

CHARLOTTE. No, just convince her this lawsuit is a subconscious reflection of her hatred for her mother and get her to call it off.

PARKER. Is that ethical?

CHARLOTTE. As one of the defendants in this lawsuit, do you care?

PARKER. (*Blinks, clears throat.*) You certainly put things bluntly.

CHARLOTTE. When you reach my age, and you're still single, you get tired of being subtle! Oh, but about Doctor Karleen's book—do you want it *now?*

PARKER. Do you know where the manuscript is?

CHARLOTTE. Yes, but let me type it up, so I get the chance to read it!

PARKER. I don't understand. It *was* typewritten.

CHARLOTTE. The casebook, yes. I'm talking about the novel. (*Hands papers to him.*) I've already fallen in love with the title.

PARKER. (*Scans topsheet, raises eyebrows, sinks slowly to sit on edge of desk.*) But— But when did Victor have the *time* to write this? We only just spoke of it *today!*

CHARLOTTE. He's a sly one, Mister Donnelly. Straight face and lovely manners, but down inside—

PARKER. (*Who has been reading with increasing fervor.*) Good heavens! This has got to be a *first* for erotic literature! Three men . . . and one woman . . . in a cement mixer—!

CHARLOTTE. Where? Where? Where? Let me see that!

PARKER. Come on over here. (*Leads way to chaise, on:*) We'll go halvsies on it!

CHARLOTTE. (*Whipping off coat and hat and depositing them across desk.*) You start reading the first bit, and I'll go make us a couple of drinks. Or is it too early in the day for you? (*Starts for cabinet.*)

PARKER. It is, but I'm willing to make an exception. All at once, it's very warm in here . . . (*Reads avidly as* CHARLOTTE *fixes drinks.*)

CHARLOTTE. Aren't you supposed to be meeting your wife for dinner and the theater?

PARKER. (*Too distracted to reply very clearly.*) Who? My wife? Oh. Yes, I suppose I am . . .

CHARLOTTE. Shouldn't you phone her or something?

PARKER. (*Manages to look up.*) What? Oh, I will, I will. But even if I don't, she'll know I'm not coming when I don't show up. Excuse me . . . This is— (*Plunges back into manuscript.*) This is a new one on me! How in the world do *three* men manage to hide from Sir Frederick, with only a—

CHARLOTTE. (*Hurrying over with drinks.*) Don't tell me! You'll spoil it! I want to read for myself!

PARKER. (*Taking drink.*) Thank you. (*Sips; then:*) Say—! I just thought . . . if Victor based this book on his case histories—

CHARLOTTE. (*Sitting beside him, taking topsheet of manuscript to read for herself.*) Don't worry, we don't have a single Jessica in the files. And I *know* we've never analyzed an English lord!

PARKER. Come to think of it, to sue for *this* kind of story, a person would have to *admit* they'd behaved like this—and *no* one is *that* crazy!

CHARLOTTE. Shut up and read!

PARKER. I'm reading, I'm reading! (*Reads a few lines; then:*) This is fantastic! Wait a minute! (*Fumbles inside coat.*) I'm not taking a chance on this getting away from us! Here— (*Takes out checkbook and pen, starts filling out check frantically.*) —this is an official publisher's advance, giving my company exclusive rights to this book, and make sure you *tell* Victor that!

CHARLOTTE. (*Looks at size of check, chokes on drink.*) Fifteen thousand dollars? What does he have to do for it?

PARKER. Just keep up the pace, page after page! Tell him he gets this now, and the same amount again on publication, and that the total of the two checks is a mere drop in the bucket of what we're *going* to make on this blockbuster!

CHARLOTTE. Oh, he'll be so pleased! Now hurry up and give me page two! This cement mixer scene has me all churned up!

PARKER. (*Hands over second sheet, scans third.*) Wait till you get to the shoot-out on the rollercoaster!

CHARLOTTE. Holy Toledo! (*Both start to read rapidly, avidly, as the CURTAIN stars slowly downward; PARKER gasps, then CHARLOTTE whistles, then PARKER chuckles, then CHARLOTTE giggles; then:*)

PARKER. (*Stares in rapt shock at page he holds.*) Oh, no! No! Who would ever have thought of such a thing!

CHARLOTTE. (*Leans to peek over his shoulder.*) Mister Donnelly, that's what *every* girl dreams of! Didn't you and Mrs. Donnelly ever—?

PARKER. (*Horrified.*) No! Never!

CHARLOTTE. Why in the world not?

PARKER. Because—well—I mean . . . (*Thinks it over; smiles.*) Hmmmmm! . . . But where can I buy a mink hammock on Saturday afternoon!?

THE CURTAIN IS DOWN

ACT TWO

Curtain rises on VICTOR'S *office/apartment again. It is
the following Wednesday afternoon.* VICTOR *is lying
supine on the chaise, an icebag covering his forehead
and eyes, his hands held firmly atop the icebag. He
is dressed somewhat better than in the preceding
act—probably in a well-tailored doublebreasted
Edwardian suit with velvet lapels and pocket-flaps.
Maybe even spats. The room is very bright and
cheery. A very faintly played recording of Ravel's
"Pavane pour Une Enfante Defunte" can be heard
on the phonograph. A moment after curtain-rise,*
CHARLOTTE—*in full nurse's uniform—enters from
anteroom, surveys* VICTOR, *shakes her head, then
moves to phonograph and stops record in mid-note.*
VICTOR *lifts icebag from face and scowls at her.*

VICTOR. Can't you let a man die in peace? Why did you
turn that off?

CHARLOTTE. The sound comes through the wall into
the reception room. You're going to send your acute depression cases right off the deep end.

VICTOR. (*Swings legs off chaise, sits up, groans and
holds icebag to top of head; then:*) I don't *have* any acute
depression cases! Except *me!*

CHARLOTTE. If your taste in music doesn't improve,
you *will* have! (*Goes to him, officiously, takes icebag.*)
Now, suck in that gut and remember how to smile. Mrs.
Melnik will be here any minute, and my salary depends
on your success with the customers.

VICTOR. (*Manages to stand groggily.*) I wish the wedding were over with. The courtship is killing me.

CHARLOTTE. (*Taking icebag up stairs to balcony door.*)
Have you ever considered *not* drinking on a date?

VICTOR. Of course I have, but I hate to come off second best with Gaby. She's an amazing woman, Miss Hennebon. Never gets tipsy, never gets fat, never gets wrinkles—

CHARLOTTE. While *you*, on the other hand—!

VICTOR. I know, I know. Remind me to burn my mirror. (*Shakes head, sways, steadies, goes to desk chair and sits, gingerly.*)

CHARLOTTE. Doctor, it's none of my business, but— You're the man. Why don't *you* call the shots? Take her to the ballet instead of a bar—

VICTOR. I don't want her to think I can't keep pace with her.

CHARLOTTE. And what do you do *after* the wedding— fix yourself some milk and cookies, switch on the Late Show, and yell "Surprise!"? (*Exits through balcony door.*)

VICTOR. (*Calls after her:*) With head like mine, you don't yell *anything!* (*Winces painfully at own shout and clutches head; while he is still sunk in misery,* ROY *enters from anteroom, affable but uneasy.*)

ROY. Oh, there you are, Victor! Have you seen Mrs. Melnik yet?

VICTOR. (*Squints at* ROY, *then carefully shakes head.*) Oh, hello, Roy. No, not yet. But you can forget about that overdose of scopolamine.

ROY. Oh. That. I was only joking. I think. Say— I understand *your* future isn't all that bleak. I hear from the grapevine that the American Psychiatric Association may have a real Hemingway on its hands.

VICTOR. (*Brightening a bit.*) Yes—that *was* a stroke of luck, wasn't it! Although I must say, I'm sorry to be— um—dancing on your grave, as it were . . .

ROY. (*Brushing it off, but unhappily.*) Timing is everything in life, Victor. Parker had an opening, and you were a perfect fit.

VICTOR. (*Bridling slightly.*) You make me sound like a *pimiento!* . . . How's the lawsuit coming?

ROY. I still don't see how Mrs. Melnik recognized herself! I didn't mention her by *name!*

VICTOR. (*Shrugs.*) Her case was probably unique!

ROY. Not *that* unique! Oh, hell, it's done, that's what counts. Nothing can save me now.

VICTOR. You missed a golden opportunity when she was still your patient. You could have *talked* her to death!

ROY. Don't kid, Vic. You're the only one can help me.

VICTOR. (*Relents a bit.*) I'll do what I can—

ROY. Anything will be appreciated. I mean—it's not just the loss of my book, my entire career's at stake! ·

VICTOR. (*Relents entirely.*) You're right! Us headshrinkers got to stick together! (PARKER *enters from anteroom, during:*)

ROY. (*Clasps* VICTOR'S *hands fervently.*) I'll never forget you for this, Victor! But what *are* you going to do when you see Mrs. Melnik?

VICTOR. Well, now, let me think . . . Oh, hi there, Park. Roy and I were just—uh—

PARKER. No details, please. I don't want to be an accessory-before-the-fact.

ROY. How about *after*-the-fact? Your car has a roomy trunk . . .

VICTOR. Maybe I can make Mrs. Melnik look on the bright side—after all, your book may have made her famous . . .

PARKER. "Notorious" is more like it.

VICTOR. Why? What's her problem?

ROY. You mean you haven't *read* my book?

VICTOR. As a matter of fact, I haven't. But even if I had, how would I know which case was Mrs. Melnik?

ROY. (*Starts for anteroom.*) I'll get you a copy.

PARKER. Roy, I told you to *burn* all your copies! (*But* ROY *exits without replying, and* PARKER *turns to* VICTOR, *on:*)

VICTOR. Never mind Roy, let's talk about *my* book!

I had hoped we could chat about it last night at Laureen's party, but you never showed up.

PARKER. My wife was indisposed.

VICTOR. Nothing serious, I hope?

PARKER. Nothing at all, really. Minor mishap. Fell out of a hammock.

VICTOR. In October?

PARKER. (*Wryly.*) It happened too quick to wait for November. (*As* VICTOR *reacts with puzzlement,* CHARLOTTE *enters—now emptyhanded—from apartment, and shuts door, then sees* PARKER *before she starts down the stairs.*)

CHARLOTTE. Oh, good afternoon, Mister Donnelly! Isn't it a lovely day? (*Descends, crosses to anteroom, during:*)

PARKER. Ah, yes! The leaves turning, the breeze quickening, the birds flying southward, and soon the delicate flutter of subpoenas into the mailbox . . . !

CHARLOTTE. Still uptight about that lawsuit?

PARKER. I *would* be, if it weren't for *Victor's* book. (*Turns to* VICTOR *as* CHARLOTTE *exits to anteroom.*) But, oh, my dear friend, have *you* given us a shot in the arm! We're going to make *millions!* And I mean that literally.

VICTOR. (*Excited, goes to liquor cabinet.*) You're serious? I could certainly use my hunk of the take . . . (*Will fix two bourbons on the rocks, during:*) You know, I can't get over the turnabout in the attitude of your board of directors. Less than a week ago, they wouldn't touch me with a ten-foot cattle-prod.

PARKER. Until now they had no notion of your genius as a writer. Oh, before I forget—I hope you don't mind—I've given your work a new title.

VICTOR. (*Coming to* PARKER *with drinks.*) You keep signing checks as big as the one you left here last week, and I'll pose *naked* for the *dust-jacket!* What are you retitling it?

PARKER. (*A bit embarrassed, hesitates, then says:*) "An Urge to Lay Bare"! Like it?

VICTOR. (*Not sure.*) Well . . .

PARKER. (*Accepts drink from* VICTOR, *who will sit in swivel chair while* PARKER *perches casually—right foot still on floor—on right edge of desk.*) It rings better than "Meanwhile, Back at the Wench . . ."

VICTOR. (*At sea, but greatly in accord.*) I won't argue that! (*Takes healthy slug of drink.*)

PARKER. But listen, the board is getting antsy about your progress.

VICTOR. What do you mean, "progress"?

PARKER. They wondered how soon you'd finish.

VICTOR. Finish what?

PARKER. Your book!

VICTOR. But Park— I *have* finished.

PARKER. Victor, you can't stop *there!* We don't even know the identity of the masked rider!

VICTOR. (*Stares at him, then stands, slowly, on:*) Park . . . one of us has gone over the brink . . . *There's* no masked rider in my book . . .

PARKER. (*Stands and faces him, perturbed.*) The hell there's *not!*

VICTOR. Now look, I wrote the book, and I ought to know—

PARKER. You can't have *forgotten—?!* Lady Jessica left her clothes and jewelry on the catwalk, and the masked rider galloped off with her emerald lavaliere while she was swimming nude in the vat of muscatel with that troupe of gypsy acrobats—?

VICTOR. *Muscatel?!*

PARKER. All right, maybe it was sherry—

VICTOR. Park, one of us is nuts. I never heard of any Lady— (*Yes, he has, and he just remembered where, on:*) —Jes-sic-a . . . ! (*A look of comprehension and dawning horror contorts his face, and then he roars toward right:*) MISS HENNEBON—!

CHARLOTTE. (*Enters at a run, halts inside doorway.*) What *is* it, Doctor? Are you all right?

VICTOR. (*Forcing himself to speak calmly but ur-

gently.) Look—last Saturday—I left some handwritten material on this desk, and I asked you to type it up for me . . .

CHARLOTTE. Yes, you did. And I typed it up.

VICTOR. And then—what did you do with it?

CHARLOTTE. Why—I—I turned it over to Mister Donnelly . . . I know it wasn't finished yet, but he was so anxious— Something's wrong!

VICTOR. (*Instantly icy calm, holds up hand, palm toward her, in imperious denial.*) No. Nothing's wrong. Everything's fine. Go back to your desk, Miss Hennebon.

CHARLOTTE. (*Retreating, uncertainly.*) Uh—all right —if you're sure there's nothing . . . ?

VICTOR. (*Smiling serenely, cool and calm.*) Nothing. Everything's fine. Dandy. Coming up roses. Go.

CHARLOTTE. Y-Yes, Doctor . . . (*Exits, leaving door open.*)

VICTOR. (*Looks after her, his smile remaining till he is sure she is out of sight and earshot; then he sits in swivel chair, facing right, and with elbows on knees, pillows face in palms, on:*) Park, I think you just bought yourself another lawsuit!

PARKER. (*Absorbs this; then:*) I think you just bought me another drink. (*Both head for cabinet, and will make and begin drinking necessary drinks, during:*) Are you telling me you *do* have a patient named Lady Jessica?

VICTOR. No, all the characters are fictional.

PARKER. Then you're telling me you've plagiarized another author's plot for this novel?

VICTOR. No. The man who wrote those pages isn't an author.

PARKER. Well, are you telling me that you've polished the work of a *would-be* writer and are claiming it as your own?

VICTOR. Of course not. This man doesn't write—I'm surprised he can *read!* He just dreams a sex novel, one chapter a night.

PARKER. (*Both have drinks, now; he is about to sip*

his, but now he pauses, curious.) Then what, may I ask, am I likely to be sued *for?*

VICTOR. (*Also stops before first sip; ponders; then:*) I'll be damned. I don't *know!* No, wait, I *do* know: *You* won't be sued, but I *will*, for breaching a privileged communication of a patient.

PARKER. He *told* you this story during a session?

VICTOR. Well, no, not exactly. We mostly talked about trading bubble-gum cards . . .

PARKER. Victor, do you realize that just *now* you *did* breach a privileged communication?

VICTOR. I can discuss a case as long as I don't name names!

PARKER. (*Slowly becoming very suave and very pleased.*) So this manuscript is not even—technically— *part* of a privileged communication, is that right?

VICTOR. (*Beginning to speculate along same lines.*) Yes, that's quite true . . . (*Snaps out of it.*) No! Wait! Stop it! I'm beginning to moralize like a *publisher!*

PARKER. (*Smoothly cajoling.*) But where's the *harm*, Vic old boy? *Your* ethics are all intact, right?

VICTOR. Not quite! Look—this patient is love-frustrated. He has vivid romantic dreams as a subconscious compensation. And *my* job is to *cure* him!

PARKER. Fine. Fine. Go ahead and cure him. What's the problem?

VICTOR. Park—once he's cured—the *dreams* stop!

PARKER. Good heavens! (*Swallows large dollop of drink.*) Then hold off curing him till the book ends!

VICTOR. But it may *never* end!

PARKER. Great! We'll run a *series!* The Jessica Books! Two volumes a year! Not just a one-shot best seller, then a life of second-string fizzles. A *family* of best sellers! Maybe more than one book in the top ten simultaneously! And you're going to throw that away for some eensy-teensy *ethics!*

VICTOR. Park, I'm a doctor—a psychiatrist! I've taken an oath! I can't let a patient go on and on in torment, when all this guy's got to do is get a girl, and he's cured!

PARKER. Victor—old friend—be reasonable— Could *any* real-life romance even *hope* to approach the kind of lovely nocturnal romantic orgies this guy is going to have for the rest of his life?

VICTOR. Well, of course not, but—

PARKER. Then aren't you *really* doing the guy a *favor* by not curing him—?

VICTOR. Well—in a certain sense—I *suppose* you could say that, but— (*Straightens, sets down empty glass on cabinet.*) *No!* I won't do it! I want my patient to throw off the shackles of neurosis, and come out into the light of day—

PARKER. —and be as miserable as the rest of us!

VICTOR. (*Strides back toward desk;* PARKER *sets own drink on cabinet and follows him.*) Do you know what you're *asking* me—?

PARKER. I'm asking you to become the richest, most famous and most important author in the history of the printing press! (*Starts slowly toward anteroom door.*) But . . . if you prefer your ethics to a Caribbean honeymoon . . .

VICTOR. (*This reaches him.*) But Park—how can I possibly square it with my conscience?

PARKER. *Now* you're worrying like a real *author!* Think it over. I'll call you later.

CHARLOTTE. (*Enters from anteroom.*) Doctor Karleen, Mrs. Melnik is here . . .

VICTOR. What—? Oh. Oh, yes. Just a moment, Miss Hennebon . . . Park—I—I'll let you know. Oh, and give my best to your wife.

PARKER. I'll have to give her second best. She'll *never* go near that *hammock* again! (*Exits past mystified* CHARLOTTE.)

CHARLOTTE. Shall I send Mrs. Melnik in, now?

VICTOR. Oh— Yes. Yes, I guess you may as well.

CHARLOTTE. Doctor . . . Is anything wrong—?

VICTOR. What could possibly be wrong? I'm going to be rich—rich—rich!

CHARLOTTE. That reminds me— Should I ask Mrs. Melnik for that fifty dollars in advance?

VICTOR. (*Unhappily airy and blasé.*) What for? Maybe I'll just start doing patients free, for kicks! Oh, don't listen to my babbling, Miss Hennebon, send her in. (*He takes wonted hand-in-jacket-pocket stance, right hand on desk, and sighs;* CHARLOTTE *meanwhile has turned to the door to the anteroom and beckons, on:*)

CHARLOTTE. This way, dear. The doctor will see you now.

(MRS. DOROTHEA MELNIK *enters; we love her at first sight; she is the epitome of every sweet little old lady we have ever seen: silver-white hair, very tiny in stature, wearing a long thin black featureless coat and a short flat featureless hat, and holding a very large black purse by its strap in her right hand; her smile is shy, her manner is hesitant but trusting, and her voice is gentle.*)

DOROTHEA. Good afternoon, doctor. It was so kind of you to see me.

CHARLOTTE. (*Charmed, reaches out toward her.*) Here, let me take your coat and hat, Mrs. Melnik . . .

DOROTHEA. (*Turns to her, smiles, says gently:*) Lay one clammy paw on me and I'll deck you, sweetheart. (*As* CHARLOTTE *recoils gingerly and makes a deft exit, shutting door, she turns back to* VICTOR, *who barely has time to hide his facial reaction and force a genial smile.*) That was Humphrey Bogart. You wanna hear Jimmy Cagney ?

VICTOR. (*Fighting to remain suave, gestures at chaise.*) Uh—perhaps a bit later. Right now, I think we should have a chat and become acquainted.

DOROTHEA. (*Opens purse, fumbles inside on:*) First things first. I've brought you something from my grandson. (*Pulls out sheaf of scribbled papers.*) Albert thought he'd give you a head start on Saturday's session.

VICTOR. (*Takes papers, stares at them, then at her.*) I didn't realize you were his grandmother?!

DOROTHEA. Would you have taken me on if he told you?

VICTOR. Uh—well—

DOROTHEA. (*Doing Cagney:*) Yoooo dirtyrat! Yoooo wouldna tookme! Yoooo wouldasaid no!

VICTOR. (*Pinches bridge of nose.*) Mrs. Melnik—if you'll just have a seat . . .

DOROTHEA. You shrinks are all alike. (*Sits on chaise.*) Invite a lady in, shut the door, get her on the couch, and then it's whoopee-time at the O. K. Corral!

VICTOR. (*Flustered, sets papers on desk, clasps hands behind back for:*) Now really, Mrs. Melnik, if we are to achieve a sound doctor-patient relationship, we are going to have to trust one another.

DOROTHEA. *I* won't tell if *you* won't . . . Hey, you wanna hear me do Greta Garbo?

VICTOR. Uh—not just now, Mrs. Melnik! Or may I call you "Dorothea"—?

DOROTHEA. My friends call me "Ro-Ro"! You know— like a boat? (*Sings happily:*) "Merrily, merrily, merrily, merrily, life is such a drag!"

VICTOR. "Life is but a *dream*" . . .

DOROTHEA. That all depends on you, Honeybunch!

VICTOR. Look—uh—Ro-Ro . . . You seem to like music . . . (*Starts for cabinet, where he will covertly fix himself a drink.*) Why don't you just sit back and relax, and I'll put something on to get you in the proper mood.

DOROTHEA. (*As she lies languorously back on chaise.*) How about a pair of pajamas? You got stripes? I dig stripes!

VICTOR. No, I *don't* got stripes! (*Recovers, pours drink, replaces bottle, on:*) But at any rate, I was talking about a record!

DOROTHEA. I don't listen to records—I *set* 'em! (*She

suddenly sits up, takes off hat, fluffs her hair a bit, then stands up and doffs coat, revealing that she is wearing a 1920s-type bathing suit, brightly colored, across which a large bathing-beauty-style satin ribbon proclaims her "Miss October, 1929"; hands on hips, she leaves coat, hat and purse on chaise, then saunters up to a point directly behind VICTOR *at the cabinet, during:*)

VICTOR. I must admit, I admire your verve and vitality —uh—Ro-Ro. It's not many women your age think of much else in life besides a rocking chair by the fireside, while they read newspaper ads trying to find a nice mausoleum for their *cat—! (Starting to sip drink, he starts to turn a bit toward chaise, and gets the full whammy of her in that outfit; he chokes violently on drink.*)

DOROTHEA. (*Pounding him efficiently on back.*) Naughty-naughty! Mustn't drink alone!

VICTOR. (*Still a bit gagged—by the drink and the view.*) Now really, Ro-Ro . . . you shouldn't run around dressed that way . . . you'll catch your death of cold . . . !

DOROTHEA. When I catch something in *this* outfit, I hope it won't be *cold! (Links arm in his, half-drags him toward chaise.*) Come on, Honeybunch, let's get all cozy on the nice couch . . .

VICTOR. (*Trying to dig in his heels and resist.*) Listen to me. Please. This isn't getting us anywhere!

DOROTHEA. You're telling me! Stop fighting!

VICTOR. (*Pulls free.*) Wait! . . . Now listen—!

DOROTHEA. I'm listening . . .

VICTOR. I'm speechless.

DOROTHEA. One cuddle is worth ten thousand words. Come on, Honeybunch—! (*Grabs for his arm; he evades her.*)

VICTOR. Look, Ro-Ro . . . Make that "Mrs. Melnik"! . . . Either you are here to seek psychiatric help or there is no point in your staying here at all. Now, much as I desire to help you with your problem—

DOROTHEA. But I haven't *told* you my problem.

VICTOR. Well, if you'll just get onto the couch . . . *alone* . . . I'll be glad to—

DOROTHEA. But if I lie down, you can't see my banner.

VICTOR. I see it, I see it! Is it a part of your problem?

DOROTHEA. I was supposed to lead the parade down Wall Street on Friday, October Thirteenth in 1929. It was my big chance. Do you know what happened?

VICTOR. Who doesn't! I can see what a traumatic disappointment that must have been. The band ready—the reporters—the photographers—and then— Wham! The bottom drops out.

DOROTHEA. No, the zipper stuck.

VICTOR. (*Absorbs this; then:*) Does Albert take after *your* side of the family?

DOROTHEA. Oh, forget about Albert, and help me with *my* problem!

VICTOR. Just exactly what *is* your problem?

DOROTHEA. (*Abruptly pinions his arms to his sides in an ardent embrace, her cheek against his chest.*) Guess!

VICTOR. (*Rolls eyes ceilingward.*) Well, I think we can rule out antisocial tendencies—! (*At this point, the anteroom door bursts open, and* CHARLOTTE—*earpieces of the stethoscope still in her ears and the chestpiece still held forward against a no-longer-present door—comes lurching into the room, and topples prone on the floor.*) Miss Hennebon! (*Then, hopefully plaintive:*) Is the hour up *already?*

(*Before* CHARLOTTE—*who props herself up with fist-and-elbow supporting her chin—can reply,* GABY, *in another dressy fall outfit, steps in from anteroom, almost stumbles over* CHARLOTTE, *then recovers balance and goes to speak to* VICTOR, *and then reacts to the tableau and gapes, and:*)

GABY. Victor! What in the world are you doing?

DOROTHEA. Analyzing his Ro-Ro!

VICTOR. Really, Gaby, you shouldn't come barging in here when I'm with a patient!

GABY. What's her problem?

CHARLOTTE. Guess!

DOROTHEA. Why don't you send these people away and put some music on?

VICTOR. Mrs. Melnik, will you kindly take your fifty dollars and get out of here!

CHARLOTTE. She hasn't *paid* her fifty dollars.

VICTOR. (*Prying himself from* DOROTHEA'S *embrace.*) Then *give* her fifty dollars! Just get her *out* of here!

GABY. Charlotte—what are you doing down there on the floor?

CHARLOTTE. I thought you'd never ask!

DOROTHEA. (*Pouting, scuffs to coat, hat and purse, on:*) Money-money-money! Nobody ever wants any *fun!*

GABY. (*Assisting* CHARLOTTE *to her feet.*) Does this sort of thing happen very often?

CHARLOTTE. Who knows? I never fell into the *room* before!

VICTOR. (*Headache-pained and enraged.*) It happens every day! Eight times a day! All my patients are sex-crazy love-goddesses, and this whole damned office is just a front for sin and vice and pagan orgies! (*Lurches for stairs.*) And *now*, if you'll excuse me, it's time for my afternoon *opium!* (*Thunders up stairs, exits to apartment, slams door after him.*)

DOROTHEA. (*Coat on but unfastened, carrying hat and purse, is just exiting past* GABY, *pauses to lay a sympathetic hand on her arm, for:*) And he *drinks*, too. (*Exits through anteroom.*)

GABY. (*After a silence.*) Victor seemed upset.

CHARLOTTE. Grooms always get nervous before the wedding.

GABY. Do *all* his sessions go like that?

CHARLOTTE. How would he find time to take notes?

GABY. (*Steps down below cabinet, faces out front, avoiding* CHARLOTTE'S *gaze, for:*) Charlotte—level with me—*who* is Lady Jessica?

CHARLOTTE. You mean the hot-blooded heroine in Doctor Karleen's book?

GABY. You know very well who I mean.

CHARLOTTE. (*Comes down to her.*) But honey—that's who she *is*—the heroine in his book. Who *else* could she be?

GABY. (*Turns to face her.*) Oh, Charlotte, I just *know* she's a real person! The Victor I knew—or thought I knew—could never *make up* such a depraved creature!

CHARLOTTE. *I* should have such a depravity!

GABY. Don't you understand? Victor's leading a double life! He—he just *has* to be!

CHARLOTTE. (*Leads her toward chaise.*) Listen, I think you'd better sit down and listen to some sensible talk from old Auntie Charlotte. No, not a word, just listen. (*Seats* GABY *on chaise, stands facing her.*) In the first place, that man up there loves you. You're all he thinks about, all he worries about, all he enjoys in this world.

GABY. But how could he—?

CHARLOTTE. Hush! Hear me out. In the second place, when in the world would that poor man have *time* to lead a double life? When he's not in here working his brain to the bone, he's out somewhere with *you!*

GABY. You can't know his *every* last move—!

CHARLOTTE. Maybe not, but that brings me to item number three: Until he got that advance from Mister Donnelly on Saturday, Doctor Karleen couldn't *afford* a double life. Hell, he couldn't afford a *single* life!

GABY. But once he had that advance—

CHARLOTTE. Honey, use your head: He got the advance *after* he'd written all that glamorous garbage. So how did he afford the double life to inspire the book that gave him the advance to afford the double life . . . ? (*Reconsiders her last statement; then:*) Did I leave the *verb* out of that sentence?

GABY. (*Wrings hands, looks away, murmurs tragically:*) Oh, Charlotte— The man who wrote that book is not the sort of man I'd planned to marry.

CHARLOTTE. I've read the book. Change your plan.

GABY. You don't understand! It's instinct—intuition— (*Stands, still wringing hands, moves with doleful solemnity toward window, on:*) You'd know in a *minute* what I meant if you were a *woman!*

CHARLOTTE. What do you *think* I am—chopped liver?!

GABY. (*This breaks her self-pity, and she turns to* CHARLOTTE, *aghast at what she has just inadvertently said.*) Oh, Charlotte, I'm sorry! I—I was sort of using you—doing a quick rehearsal of what I intend to say to Victor—and I forgot you weren't him!

CHARLOTTE. It's the stethoscope—fools everybody.

GABY. (*Comes to her, takes her hands.*) Tell me— honestly—what am I going to do?

CHARLOTTE. All right, I *will* tell you. You're going to stop all this idiotic self-pity, and be your brightest and cheeriest when Doctor Karleen feels guilty enough to come back out here, and then you are going to marry him on schedule and forget all these imbecilic notions! Doctor Karleen is one of the sweetest— (*For first time, notices latest set of dream papers on desk.*) Hey, look, he's been at it again! (*Rushes to desk, grabs up papers.*) I've *got* to find out the identity of the mysterious masked rider!

GABY. And that's *another* thing! You say all he does is see patients and take me out—when does he find time to write that damned novel?! How does he get any sleep?

CHARLOTTE. What makes you think he *does?* Have you seen his *eyes* lately? They look like rosebudded radishes! (*Looks at topsheet of manuscript, gasps.*) I'll be damned! The masked rider is a woman!

GABY. (*Rushes to peer over her shoulder.*) That's impossible! What woman? What's her name?

CHARLOTTE. Wait, let me look! Ah! It says her name is— (*Turns page to next sheet, stares open-mouthed; then she and* GABY *turn their heads until they are facing one another, and speak in incredulous unity:*)

GABY and CHARLOTTE. "Charlotte Hennebon!"?

GABY. (*Takes backstep, points shocked finger.*) You mean that *you* are Victor's double life? *You? YOU?*

CHARLOTTE. Now, just a minute, it's not all *that* ridiculous!

GABY. But Charlotte—I mean—you—and Victor—! (*Starts to laugh, despite herself.*)

CHARLOTTE. (*Hands on hips, surveys her a moment; then:*) If this wasn't good therapy for you, kiddo, I think I'd bean you with the nearest blunt instrument!

GABY. (*Recovering in fits and starts.*) Oh . . . I'm sorry . . . really, I am . . . it's just that the idea is so . . . is so . . .

CHARLOTTE. All *right* already! That's therapeutic enough for one day! I may not be a Hollywood starlet, but I'm not exactly ready to be recycled, either! . . . (*At this moment, ROY enters from anteroom; he is in homburg and overcoat, and carries a small suitcase; his manner is uneasy and harried.*)

ROY. Oh, hi! Where's Victor? Upstairs? Never mind, I'll find him. (*Starts toward stairs.*)

CHARLOTTE. If that's a change of clothes for Mrs. Melnik, her ship just sailed.

ROY. (*On stairs.*) It's pajamas and underwear. I thought I'd move in with Victor for a few days.

CHARLOTTE. I'd knock gently if I were you. He's still in post-Melnik shock.

ROY. Oh. Then you've *met* her. Quite an experience, isn't she!

CHARLOTTE. I haven't decided. She's never *did* get around to Greta Garbo.

ROY. Well, I tried to warn you about her—

CHARLOTTE. The hell you did. You danced around on one foot screaming "Ethics!" and "Bodysnatcher!"

GABY. Is *she* what they were squabbling about last Saturday?

ROY. Now, Charlotte, be fair. How *could* I tell Victor about her, without breaching the doctor/patient relationship?

GABY. You couldn't tell *Victor*, but you *could* tell forty thousand readers?

ROY. That's different!

GABY. Why?

CHARLOTTE. He got paid for it!

ROY. Oh, c'mon, give me a break. *Is* Victor in?

CHARLOTTE. If he hasn't stepped off the terrace. But, Doctor Terrigan—why *are* you here, so suddenly and all?

ROY. Because there is a process server on his way up from the lobby to my apartment, and I don't want that subpoena till I've had a chance to prepare my defense.

GABY. How do you know he's on the way up?

ROY. The doorman phoned me.

CHARLOTTE. But how did he know this guy was a process server?

GABY. Yes. They don't carry a sign or anything.

ROY. He's the doorman's brother.

GABY. He betrayed his own brother out of loyalty to a tenant?

ROY. Loyalty has nothing to do with it. His brother doesn't tip him twenty bucks at Christmas! (*Raps lightly at balcony door.*) Victor? Victor, may I see you a moment?

GABY. (*Waves hand at manuscript* CHARLOTTE *holds.*) Get that out of sight! Victor mustn't know I've been sneak-previewing his book.

CHARLOTTE. Hey, that's right! (*Scurries to exit into dressing room.*)

ROY. (*Raps again.*) *Yo, Vic!?*

VICTOR. (*Off.*) Who is it?

ROY. It's Roy. Roy Terrigan.

VICTOR. (*Off.*) No, thanks, I already *have* a headache.

ROY. Aw, Vic, cut it out, please! This is an emergency.

VICTOR. (*Opens door, comes out, leaving door ajar.*) Ro-Ro sends her love! (*Sees suitcase.*) What've you brought me *now* . . . her favorite *records?!* (*Sees* GABY, *still below desk.*) You're still here! I'm glad. I was afraid

I'd find your engagement ring lying on the desk . . . wired to a hand grenade.

GABY. I understand, darling. That woman would upset anybody.

VICTOR. I don't deserve you.

ROY. Look, if you two want to play the balcony scene, I'll just sneak out of your way . . . (*Starts into apartment.*)

VICTOR. Hold it! (ROY *stops.*) Where do you think you're going?

ROY. Victor—old friend—I didn't think you'd mind sharing your bed with me for a few nights . . .

VICTOR. Is your teddy bear in the wash *again?!*

GABY. Victor, it *is* an emergency—there's a man with a subpoena looking for him. He needs a temporary hideout. (CHARLOTTE *enters from dressing room, no longer carrying the dream-manuscript.*)

ROY. Just until I've prepared my defense.

VICTOR. What's wrong with *insanity?*

GABY. Roy's not insane.

CHARLOTTE. But Mrs. Melnik sure is! I'm ashamed of you, Doctor Terrigan. The least you could've done was have Doctor Karleen bone up on his karate!

ROY. Against a kleptomaniac? All she does is heist other people's property.

GABY. What ever happened to privileged communications?

ROY. Well, you all seemed to *know* her problem . . .

VICTOR. Roy, the only item Mrs. Melnik tried to heist was *me!*

CHARLOTTE. Yeah, where did you get this kleptomaniac notion?

ROY. Wait, I forgot this isn't September anymore.

GABY. What's that got to do with it?

ROY. She changes aberrations monthly. When she first came to me in July, she had a father-fixation. Then in August, she showed up with every last twitch of the classic manic-depressive syndrome. September, she began filching things—jewelry from department stores, note-pads from my desk, umbrellas from restaurants— What is she doing *now?*

CHARLOTTE. Playmate of the Month.

VICTOR. (*Fingertips to forehead, eyes wide.*) Hold on—! The Great Detective is about to speak! Mrs. Melnik lives with Albert . . . Albert reads the Readers Digest . . . The Readers Digest is chockful of self-analysis tests . . . !

GABY. Good, grief, that's *it!* Mrs. Melnik is the October Issue Test Maniac!

CHARLOTTE. Well, that's Life in These United States!

ROY. Look, all this conjecture is fascinating as hell, but—

VICTOR. Oh, go, boy, go! Make yourself at home, then come back with a good hangover recipe. (ROY *exits with suitcase into apartment.*)

GABY. Victor, have you been drinking again?

VICTOR. Not again. Still. It doesn't bother you evenings, why should it bother you days?

GABY. You don't have to bite my head off.

VICTOR. I'm sorry.

GABY. No you're not.

VICTOR. All right, I'm not!

CHARLOTTE. I can see you two lovebirds would rather be alone . . . (*Starts toward anteroom, but stops on:*)

GABY. Never mind, Charlotte, I was just going! (*Sails past* CHARLOTTE *out anteroom door.*)

VICTOR. (*Rushing down from balcony, around desk, toward anteroom, etc.*) Gaby, wait! Listen to reason! It's just premarital nerves! I've been in a tight squeeze—

GABY. (*Pops back into room on:*) The kind you get from Ro-Ro?

VICTOR. (*Stops rushing below chaise.*) I don't believe it! You're jealous of a seventy-five-year-old bathing beauty?

GABY. It's not just that! What about Charlotte?

VICTOR. *Charlotte?!*

GABY. Yeah! You know! The masked rider! Or was that secret identity just a coincidence?!

CHARLOTTE. He just needed a name in a hurry. I've only been on a horse once in my life, and it made me throw up.

GABY. Oh, I'm not blaming *you*, Charlotte.

CHARLOTTE. Personally, I blame the horse.

VICTOR. May *I* get a word in edgewise?

GABY. No! And until you *do* decide the name of the reigning woman in (*She struggles to tug off a ring.*) your life, you can take your engagement ring and—and—you can just—!

CHARLOTTE. Want a little soap?

GABY. I'll mail it to you! (*Turns to storm out of room, stops dead as* JINGLE JABONSKI *strides in;* JINGLE *is about 25 years old, in blue jeans and a floppy sweatshirt and sneakers, her hair in a very impromptu ribbon-bowed ponytail.*)

JINGLE. Hi! Have you got something green and shiny?

CHARLOTTE. Yes, but it won't come off her finger.

GABY. Oh, get out of my way, all of you! (*Sweeps imperiously past* JINGLE *and exits.*)

VICTOR. Young lady—

JINGLE. Hi! You must be Doctor Karleen. Your name was on the bell-button. I'm Jingle Jabonski. I live in the apartment next door.

CHARLOTTE. If you're the Welcome Wagon, you missed the boat.

JINGLE. Naw, I'm on a scavenger hunt. I need something green and shiny, and I figured that, Doctor Karleen being a psychiatrist, he'd have a rubber plant!

VICTOR. (*Goes to her as she goes to rubber plant.*) Young lady, I admire your neighborly spirit, but you can't just come exploding into my office and— (*As she turns to look curiously at him, he stops to think a moment; then:*) How did you know I had a rubber plant?

JINGLE. You're a headshrinker, aren't you?

CHARLOTTE. If you want a polite answer, you'd better rephrase that.

JINGLE. (*Smacks forehead with palm.*) Boy, am I ever a dope! Psychiatrist! That better? I keep forgetting you medical people never keep in touch with the language.

VICTOR. Now, wait—I *know* what a "headshrinker" is!

JINGLE. (*Surveys him, hands on hips.*) Then what's your beef?

CHARLOTTE. (*To* VICTOR.) Yeah, what's your beef?

VICTOR. Miss Jabonski . . . !

JINGLE. Aw, c'mon, call me "Jingle"! It's more neighborly!

VICTOR. (*Stiffening.*) *Miss Jabonski—!*

CHARLOTTE. Oh, stop it, both of you! *I* want to know how she knew you'd have a rubber plant!

JINGLE. Doctors *always* have a rubber plant. Except in the tropics.

VICTOR. Why not in the tropics?

JINGLE. Rubber plants *live* in the tropics. What would it prove?

CHARLOTTE. What does it prove in *this* climate?

JINGLE. The rubber plant sends a subliminal message to the patients. When they walk in and find it thriving nicely despite the hostile climate outside, they know they can trust the doctor.

VICTOR. (*Despite himself.*) What message?

JINGLE. That motto of Hippocrates, Father of Modern Medicine: "If a rubber plant can do it, so can you!"

VICTOR. Hippocrates said no such thing!

JINGLE. Then why've you got a rubber plant?

VICTOR. The florist was all out of *Brussels Sprouts!*

JINGLE. (*Sizes him up for one beat; then:*) I think I could fall for a guy like you. (*As* VICTOR *gapes, breezily changes topic.*) Well, do I get the rubber plant or don't I?

VICTOR. (*Dazed by her verbal footwork.*) Why are you on a scavenger hunt at three in the afternoon?

JINGLE. Why *not?* Now, c'mon, yes or no, I've got a parlorful of guests waiting.

CHARLOTTE. Why aren't *they* out scavenging?

JINGLE. They were. But nobody got anything green and shiny. If I get the rubber plant, I win.

VICTOR. Oh, take it, take it!

JINGLE. That's a pretty big pot. I'd better get a dolly. (*Starts for anteroom door.*)

VICTOR. Just try to get it back here without too much root shock.

JINGLE. (*Turns, scans him; then:*) Do you believe in love at first sight?

VICTOR. Love at first sight is a ridiculous romantic aspiration. No emotionally mature adult believes in such a thing.

JINGLE. Yeah, but do *you?*

VICTOR. Miss Jabonski—!

JINGLE. Call me "Jingle"! (*Exits through anteroom door.*)

VICTOR. How did a girl like that get on Park Avenue?!

CHARLOTTE. Hell, *you're* on Park Avenue . . . ! (*The PHONE rings.*)

VICTOR. (*Goes toward desk.*) I'll get it!

CHARLOTTE. Who's arguing? (*Goes over to rubber plant, idly inspects its leaves, musing.*)

VICTOR. (*On phone.*) Hello? . . . Parker! How are you! . . . The what—? . . . You're kidding! . . . When, today? . . . But the book's not even finished—! . . .

(ALBERT *enters from anteroom, unnoticed, in topcoat, distraught; he carries a rolled-up Readers Digest in his right hand; he stops just inside doorway, itching to speak, but too polite to move further or say a word while* VICTOR *is on the phone.*)

CHARLOTTE. (*Straightening from plant, observes:*) I wonder if Hippocrates *did* have a rubber plant?

VICTOR. (*On phone.*) Yes, sir, you bet! . . . As fast as possible! . . . Don't worry about a thing . . . Wait'll I tell Gaby, she'll flip! . . . Talk to you later! (*Hangs *up, starts toward* CHARLOTTE, *moving right past* ALBERT *without really noticing him except perfunctorily, during:*) Miss Hennebon, guess what's happened! That was Parker on the phone! (*She turns as he continues:*) On the strength of just the first few chapters, my book's been selected by the Book of the Month Club, a major Hollywood studio is dickering for the motion picture rights, and Park's board of directors is pulling strings to get me nominated for the Pulitzer Prize!—Oh, hi there, Albert!— Can you *imagine*, Miss Hennebon—?! (*Realizes.*) *Albert?!* (*Spins to face him.*) It's you! You're here! Boy, am I glad to see *you!* Just when I need you most, you beautiful dreamer!

ALBERT. I can't stay.

VICTOR. But you've *got* to stay!

CHARLOTTE. Albert, I thought you couldn't get here in the middle of the week?

ALBERT. This is an emergency! Where's my grandmother?!

VICTOR. I'm afraid she's already left. Now, listen, Albert—

ALBERT. But her hour's not up! Was she here a full hour?

VICTOR. It sure *seemed* like an hour! Anyhow, the important thing is, *you're here*, and—

ALBERT. But I've got to *find* her! Have you seen this month's issue of Readers Digest? (*Waves it at him.*)

VICTOR. What is that—the November issue?

ALBERT. It just hit the stands! Grandmother mustn't see it!

VICTOR. (*Suddenly catching his drift.*) Wait a minute— Let *me* see it! (*Grabs it, looks, gasps.*) Oh, no!

CHARLOTTE. What's wrong?

VICTOR. (*Holds it before her, points at place, and simultaneously reads aloud:*) "Are You Suicide-Prone?"!

CHARLOTTE. I don't *think* so . . .

ALBERT. No-no, my *grandmother* takes these tests! And

she always *passes!* I've got to go *find* her! (*Starts for door,* VICTOR *grabs his arm.*)

VICTOR. Now, now, calm yourself, Albert. What you need is a nice healthy physicial examination!

CHARLOTTE. A *what?!*

VICTOR. (*Gesturing regally.*) Miss Hennebon, will you kindly prepare the examination room? (*Starts trying to undo* ALBERT'S *necktie.*)

CHARLOTTE. (*Half-step toward dressing room; then:*) What do you mean—open the door and turn on the light?

ALBERT. But I don't need a physical! I've got to find my grandmother! (*Takes necktie—it's a clip-on—hands it to* VICTOR.) Goodbye!

VICTOR. (*Grabs* ALBERT'S *arm again.*) Oh, never mind, Miss Hennebon, I'll handle this myself! (*Leads* ALBERT *toward dressing room.*) Come along, Albert. I'm going to make you well again! (*Exits with* ALBERT *into dressing room, shuts door.*)

CHARLOTTE. (*To no one in particular.*) *One* of those two is off his *nut!* . . . Or *I* am! (GABY *enters from anteroom; her manner is now controlled, and her attitude semi-contrite.*)

GABY. Charlotte! My dear sweet friend!

CHARLOTTE. Or *she* is!

GABY. . . . What?

CHARLOTTE. Nothing. It's been one of those days. Are you feeling better now, Miss Wingate?

GABY. I've decided to forgive Victor.

CHARLOTTE. Considering he didn't do anything, that's mighty big of you.

GABY. I *was* rather shrewish, wasn't I! Premarital nerves, I guess.

CHARLOTTE. What are you two using for an alibi *after* the wedding?

GABY. (*Impatiently.*) Is Victor *here?* I'd really like to see him now, if you don't mind.

CHARLOTTE. He's giving a patient a complete physical

examination, but I'm sure he won't be long. Albert's not very big. (*Exits to anteroom.*)

GABY. (*As the name registers, calls after her.*) You don't mean Mister Brock—? I thought he could only get here on Saturdays?

CHARLOTTE. (*Off.*) Then *you* haven't seen the latest *Readers Digest!*

GABY. What's Readers Digest got to do with it?

CHARLOTTE. (*Off.*) Search *me!*

(*As* GABY *tries to figure this out,* ROY—*now elegant in one of* VICTOR'S *fanciest dressing gowns, with complementary silken scarf—steps out of apartment onto balcony, with tall glass of something like tomato juice in his hand.*)

ROY. Well, here's that hangover recipe—but where's Victor?

GABY. Roy! You're just the person I want to see! (*Moves around desk, and will join him on balcony.*)

ROY. *Now* you're talking!

GABY. I mean professionally!

ROY. What *profession?*

GABY. Please be serious! I'm terribly worried about Victor!

ROY. Well, come inside and let *Victor* worry about *you!*

GABY. (*Now on balcony with him, before open door.*) Oh, Roy, please don't clown around, this is important!

ROY. Say, you *are* upset. Your mascara's an unholy mess. Been crying? . . . Or is this hangover remedy for *you?*

GABY. (*Looks at glass.*) What's in it?

ROY. Nothing we can't pour down the bathroom sink while we switch to martinis! Come on inside. (*Gestures toward apartment.*) I promise not to bite you.

GABY. Thank you. (*Starts into apartment.*)

ROY. However, I won't promise not to bite you *back!*

(*Straightens scarf with one hand, stands tall, and follows her into apartment, closing door.*)

(*A second later,* VICTOR *leans out of dressing room.*)

VICTOR. Miss Hennebon!
CHARLOTTE. (*Hurrying in from anteroom.*) Yes, Doctor?
VICTOR. Come in here, I need your help! I can't get the knots out of Albert's shoelaces!

(CHARLOTTE *hurries into dressing room,* VICTOR *pops back inside with her and shuts door; a moment later,* DOROTHEA, *carrying an open copy of Readers Digest and reading from it, strolls in from anteroom, humming pleasantly but more-or-less tunelessly; she goes to desk, sets magazine down in open position, and as she reads, removes her hat and coat and folds the coat into a neat bundle; then she goes to spot between bookcase and window, sets bundled coat on floor, lays her purse flat on top of that, then sets hat at apex of the stack; then she opens the window as far up as it will go, returns to desk, takes up magazine again, and—still reading and humming— carefully clambers out window in her bathing suit, balances on what must be a ledge outside the window, then—still reading and humming—sidles toward downstage left and out of our view; a moment after this,* CHARLOTTE *comes out of dressing room, carrying* ALBERT'S *bundled clothing, his shoes on top, and* VICTOR *steps out, too, and shuts door after him.*)

CHARLOTTE. Doctor, I don't understand . . . Why don't we just hang these up?
VICTOR. (*Keeping his voice low, lest* ALBERT *hear.*) Miss Hennebon, I'm afraid that unless we act quickly, and a bit unorthodoxly, Albert will be in very grave mental trouble. He *must* remain here, in these quarters,

for at least a week, perhaps longer. Without his clothing, he obviously cannot go anywhere.

CHARLOTTE. But he can't spend a week standing behind that screen—!

VICTOR. I'll let him out as soon as you've put his clothing in my bedroom closet. Now, move!

CHARLOTTE. Do you want any assistance with his physical?

VICTOR. There won't be any. That was a ruse, to get his clothes! But I *do* want you to bring my tape recorder in here. Then you may leave for the whole week, with pay.

CHARLOTTE. But what about your other appointments?

VICTOR. Cancel them. I can't leave Albert. He may go to sleep at any minute!

CHARLOTTE. Well . . . he's *dressed* for it! (*Shrugs, starts for stairs to apartment, sees* DOROTHEA'S *effects by open window.*) Doctor, whose are these?

VICTOR. Whose are what?

CHARLOTTE. These things by the open window—say, did *you* leave that window open?

VICTOR. In October? Don't be an idiot! Shut that before they increase my heating bill!

CHARLOTTE. (*Sets* ALBERT'S *clothing on floor beside* DOROTHEA'S *things, straightens, reaches for window, then looks back at things.*) Doctor—isn't that *Mrs. Melnik's* topcoat and hat?

VICTOR. Now, what would Mrs. Melnik's things be doing by an open window—? (*Realizes exactly what, on:*) Oh, no! She didn't! She wouldn't! Not from *my* office! (*Has bolted across room for a look out window, stops, looks left, then looks right, and:*) Mrs. Melnik! Are you crazy? It's thirteen floors to the street! (*Outside window, POLICE SIREN begins, grows louder.*)

CHARLOTTE. Maybe she's not superstitious.

VICTOR. Don't be brilliant! Go out there and *get* her! (*Shoves her halfway out window, on:*)

CHARLOTTE. Who, *me?* I get dizzy in *French heels!*

(*As they argue,* JINGLE *strides jauntily in from anteroom, waves at* CHARLOTTE *on:*)

JINGLE. I couldn't find a dolly. I'll have to drag the thing. (*Goes to rubber plant, bends, starts moving backward along front of cabinet, pulling pot, her hip pockets leading the way, just as* ALBERT, *in nothing but boxer shorts, comes curiously out of dressing room, his gaze toward window, just as* JINGLE *bumps cabinet, and it begins to play, at peak volume, a recording of Tchaikovsky's "Romeo and Juliet" love-theme, just like when lovers realize they are looking at their lovers in the movies; and as the music soars and swells,* ALBERT *turns and stares at* JINGLE'S *rearmost portions, and* JINGLE *slowly senses the stare and stands erect and then turns and looks into* ALBERT'S *face, and then, as* VICTOR *turns from window at sound of music and sees to his horror what is occurring,* ALBERT *and* JINGLE— *walking like zombies, start toward one another with arms open for an ardent embrace, faces aglow with the discovery of love, and:*)

VICTOR. No, Albert, no! (*Rushes madly across room toward him.*) Don't look at that girl! You mustn't! You're not all dreamed out, yet!

DOROTHEA. (*Appears at open window.*) Turn down that music! I can't hear the sirens! (*As* VICTOR *inserts himself between a converging* ALBERT *and* JINGLE, CHARLOTTE *lunges at* DOROTHEA *and tries to wrestle her in through the window, just as* GABY *and* ROY *pop out of apartment onto balcony to see what the ruckus is, and* VICTOR—*looking ardently into* JINGLE'S *face—while holding* ALBERT *off, hand to his chest—exclaims:*)

VICTOR. You were right! I knew I didn't fool you! It *was* love at first sight! Kiss me! Hold me! Take me! Just leave Albert alone!

GABY. Victor, what are you saying?!

VICTOR. (*In mid-embrace with a stunned-but-delighted* JINGLE, *turns head to roar over shoulder:*) How many times have I *told* you: *Don't* interrupt me during *busi-*

ness hours!! (*And as* VICTOR *and* JINGLE *go into glorious clinch and smooch, and* GABY *screams, flings her arms overhead and faints backward into a pleased* ROY'S *arms—*)

THE CURTAIN FALLS

ACT THREE

Curtain rises on VICTOR'S *office/apartment. It is a few hours later, early evening. Window is closed, drapes are drawn,* DOROTHEA'S *garments are no longer on floor, rubber plant and pot are gone, lighting is somewhat subdued to artificial rather than daylight brightness, though very bright in area of armchair because lamp is turned on behind it; when any of the doors are opened, the areas beyond them will be lighted but similarly subdued to that same artificial-lighting level. Where the rubber plant stood, the folding stepladder—closed—stands leaning against the wall. The mobile is no longer hanging from the ceiling, but is still visible: It is half-in-half-out of wastebasket right of desk. The floorstand ashtray, heaped high with cigarette butts, has been moved to a spot just in front of the right arm of the armchair.* VICTOR *is seated in armchair, taking a final fitful puff on a cigarette; he will blow out a plume of smoke, then grind out the cigarette in the tray a moment after curtain-rise.* ALBERT, *swathed and tucked into a large blanket—under which he is dressed as at the close of Act Two—lies on chaise, eyes closed.* PARKER *is seated on file cabinet, facing right, legs dangling, hunched forward, his folded arms elbow-braced upon his knees. Both he and* VICTOR *are jacketless and tieless; their jackets and ties are hanging on the coat tree left of the anteroom door. The mood is akin to that of a long wake, after the small talk has run out. The silence hangs heavy until* VICTOR *has finished grinding out his cigarette; then he dusts off his fingers and raises up a bit for a peep at* ALBERT. PARKER *sees the movement and straightens from his slouch, and then speaks softly:*

PARKER. Well?

VICTOR. (*Impatiently but softly.*) Well what?

PARKER. Any sign of rapid eye movements?

VICTOR. How can I possibly tell from here?

PARKER. Why don't you lean over his face and look?

VICTOR. Because my panicky breathing might wake him up!

PARKER. Now, look, Victor, we've got to keep calm about this thing . . .

VICTOR. With my engagement on the rocks, my career in fatal jeopardy, and financial ruin sending out an R.S.V.P?!

PARKER. *Ssh!* You'll wake him up!

ALBERT. (*Without moving or opening his eyes.*) I'm not asleep.

VICTOR. (*Jumps irritably to his feet.*) You mean you've just been lying there *awake* for the past half hour?

ALBERT. (*Now opens eyes, squirms onto his side, the better to look up at* VICTOR.) Well, everytime I move or talk, you whimper.

PARKER. (*Hops off file cabinet, crosses toward right.*) I can't stand it! I'm going to have a drink!

ALBERT. I even tried moving my eyes rapidly, but nothing happened. All I saw were blobs of color.

VICTOR. Albert, when a sleeping person starts to *dream,* rapid eye movements start by *themselves,* readily discernible through the eyelids. But you *can't* work it *backwards!*

PARKER. (*Getting bottle out of cabinet.*) Will you join me? This offer may not be repeated tonight— The supply is getting low.

VICTOR. Oh, hell, I may as well!

ALBERT. Can I have my Jingle, now?

VICTOR. (*Slouching toward* PARKER.) No, you can not! I told you why I kissed her—to keep her from throwing herself at you. It's important to your therapy, Albert. I'm your doctor. Trust me.

ALBERT. But if my problem is not having a girl, and now I can get one—?

VICTOR. Not until you've dreamed the final chapter! You've got to get all that frustration out of your system. Dream the ending, and then you can have your Jingle.

PARKER. (*As* ALBERT *settles back with a sigh, speaks* sotto voce *to* VICTOR:) Do you think it's going to work, Victor? *Can* you con a man into dreaming-to-specification?

VICTOR. Who knows? By threatening to withhold Miss Jabonski until he finishes the damned book, I might just trigger his subconscious!

PARKER. I can't stand the waiting. Those last four chapters are some of the most stupendous writing I've ever encountered in my career as a publisher— But how does the damned thing come out?!

VICTOR. (*Accepting drink from* PARKER.) If he can bring it off, it should really be a pip! I've never been so racked with suspense in my life!

(*For next five speeches, each man will say his speech, then sip as the other says his, and vice-versa, in rhythmical alternation.*)

PARKER. Yeah! *Will* Sir Frederick find the missing lavaliere in Sidney's underwear drawer—?

VICTOR. Will the Masked Rider's secret identity be revealed *before* the hurricane reaches the beach house—?

PARKER. Who's the *real* father of Lavinia's triplets—?

VICTOR. Which one of the gypsy acrobats sent the cement mixer up onto the rollercoaster in the *first* place—?

PARKER. And most important of all . . . after three reckless flirtations, seven fiendish murders, five torrid love affairs, and countless moonlight rendezvouses—

VICTOR. (*Echoing prounuciation:*) "—voozes"?

PARKER. Okay, "vooz"! Who cares? But after all these carryings-on, will Lady Jessica find true love at last?!

ALBERT. And how will she *recognize* it?!

VICTOR. (*Quietly.*) Shut *up*, Albert . . .

ALBERT. But how *will* she?

PARKER. Her *heart* will know! Okay?

ALBERT. But—

VICTOR. Go to sleep. Like a good boy. Please. Dream your dream, write it down, the cure's complete, and I'll surrender Miss Jabonski.

ALBERT. I can't. I just can't. I've tried, but I can't. When my grandmother's not here to sing to me—

PARKER. Now, now, the moment Miss Hennebon gets your grandmother sprung from stir, she'll whisk her right back here to you.

ALBERT. Grandmother's never been arrested before.

VICTOR. Well, *anyone* wearing a banner emblazoned with "October 1929" on it, who climbs onto a window ledge, is *bound* to stir up a *little* suspicion.

PARKER. That reminds me—I liked the quick-thinking way you told that policeman she was simply acting out a therapeutic psycho-drama!

VICTOR. Did you like the quick-thinking way he asked me to help him spell it?

PARKER. Well, I'm sure his lieutenant downtown will be more sympathetic. Your average policeman doesn't understand the techniques of modern psychiatry.

ALBERT. Yeah. He sees a woman on a ledge looking at Readers Digest, he figures she's a nut!

VICTOR. Albert, much as I enjoy your brilliant companionship, I do wish you'd settle back and try for that final dream . . .

ALBERT. Okay, I'll try. But it's not much use without my grandmother . . . (*As he settles back and shuts his eyes,* ROY *comes out apartment door garbed and laden as when he first arrived to move in—homburg, overcoat, suitcase; he descends stairs as* VICTOR *and* PARKER *drain their drinks and set glasses on cabinet; they watch him cross to anteroom door without a word, then hesitate short of grasping the knob.*)

Roy. *You* better open it, Vic.

Victor. No way, buddy. All you've got to worry about running into is a process server or Mrs. Melnik. *I* have Miss *Gabrielle Wingate* to steer clear of.

Parker. You say she left under strained circumstances . . . where do you suppose she went?

Victor. Probably the nearest hardware store. She managed to tear down her mobile with her bare hands, (*Appropriate gestures at mobile and mural.*) but that mural's gonna take a hammer and chisel! . . . I could kill the guy who sold me this rotten phonograph!

Parker. Well, you couldn't know a random thump would turn the music on.

Albert. It was just like in the movies!

Victor. *Damn it all to hell, go to sleep!*

Roy. Vic, would you please just sneak a *peek* outside this door . . . ?

Victor. Oh, all right, Roy!

Parker. (*As* Victor *moves toward door.*) Say, Roy, I'm puzzled about something— After Vic described Mrs. Melnik's case to me—that maniac-of-the-month thing— I looked all through your book and couldn't find a case anything even *remotely* resembling that—

Victor. (*Has opened door a fraction, peeked out, and now opens it wide, on:*) All clear!

Roy. (*To* Parker:) I know what you mean, Park! Beats me, too. I mean, what she's *suing* for. I didn't *know* about the maniac-of-the-month hangup, of course, when I was *writing* the book. (*As they chat, behind them, unnoticed,* Albert *will get more comfortable, curl up, and sleep.*)

Victor. I only guessed the problem after I'd gone through my first session with *Albert,* when he mentioned Readers Digest. Say, I just thought of something— Her case is not *unique*—*!*

Parker. Maniac-of-the-month isn't *unique?!*

Victor. I mean, her various cases—individually—were *classical* hangups! Standards. They could be anybody's!

Roy. (*Catches on, removes hat in growing elation.*) Vic, that's *it!* No matter *which* case she claims as hers, I can prove to the presiding magistrate that somebody *else* had a father-fixation, or a manic-depressive syndrome, or—!

Parker. Hey—that's right! The judge will *have* to find in your favor!

Roy. Then what am I *running* for?! (*Over next few lines he will remove overcoat and hat, hang them on coat tree, and leave suitcase near base of coat tree.*) Parker, I think we're free and clear! My book can go right back onto the shelves—Christmas is coming—all those lovely royalties start pouring in again—

Victor. Now wait a minute—! Park, you said that *my* book would outsell Roy's by millions—!

Parker. *Your* book? *What* book? Fourteen earth-shattering chapters and no *finish?*

Victor. But if you'll just let Albert have that final dream—

Roy. What has *Albert* got to do with Victor's book?

Parker. (*Realizes he and* Victor *have said too much.*) Uh . . . why . . . one last case history. A smasheroo.

Victor. Albert—uh—has some very interesting dreams. One more should wind up the book in spectacular fashion.

Parker. And then— Book of the Month, movie rights, a Pulitzer Prize . . .

Roy. (*Concerned, but trying not to show it.*) Is that a fact . . . (*Then notices:*) Hey! I think Albert's actually gone to sleep! (*Then, as* Victor *and* Parker *rush up on tiptoe to gaze raptly down at* Albert's *smiling face:*) Me and my big mouth!

Victor. (*To* Roy:) Ssh! Not a sound!

Parker. (*Whispering:*) He slipped off so fast—! What do you suppose did the trick?

Victor. *Roy* was talking—that would put *anybody* to sleep! (Roy *bridles, then looks at phonograph, then edges stealthily toward it during:*) Look, Park, look! Rapid eye movements! He's dreaming! This may be it!

PARKER. Keep your voice down, you numbskull!

VICTOR. You're noisier than I am! (*At which point* ROY, *backed against phonograph, kicks it into life with his heel, full volume, with a spirited rendition, by a large brass band, of "Stars and Stripes Forever"; as* VICTOR *and* PARKER *nearly jump through the ceiling,* ALBERT *sits up in aroused shocked, blinking and gasping, while* ROY *turns his head innocently toward the phonograph, as though it had activated without his help. Spinning to face* ROY.) Turn that damned thing *off!*

PARKER. (*As* ROY *not-too-swiftly does so, to* ALBERT:) Easy, boy, easy! Did you finish the *dream?* Did you? *Did you?!*

ALBERT. I—I—I—!

VICTOR. (*Whirling back to* ALBERT, *grasping him by the shoulders in gentle frenzy.*) Don't panic! You'll lose all the details! Never mind us! Just hang onto that dream, Albert! Think! Tell us!

ALBERT. (*A little calmer.*) L-Lady Jessica . . . she finally confessed everything to her husband . . . and the shock of hearing the truth knocked him dead . . .

PARKER. Beautiful, beautiful, beautiful—!

VICTOR. Shut up! He'll forget *everything!*

ALBERT. . . . so she inherited all his money, his estate in Surrey, his polo ponies, his oil stock . . .

PARKER. Never mind the legacy! What about the *sex?!*

ALBERT. And she found her true love at last! A man named—named—

VICTOR. *Who,* Albert, *who—!?*

ALBERT. (*About to reply, stops, thinks, seems puzzled by his own answer, and says—his inflextion a statement, but also very dubious question:*) John Philip Sousa—*!?*

VICTOR. (*Clenches fingers into hair at temples, on:*) Aaaaaaarghhhh! (*Spins to glare maniacally at phonograph.*) *You* did this! *You,* you stupid machine! (*On each word, he advances stiff-legged toward the phonograph, not even seeing* ROY, *who is being cautious enough to cower right of ladder.*) I'll tear out your woofers! I'll grind my heel in your tweeters! (*At this moment,* GABY *strides in from anteroom with a hammer and chisel;* VICTOR *grabs one in each hand.*) Thank you! Stand back! I'm about to end the Industrial Age!

PARKER. (*Just before* VICTOR *can bring down hammer onto the cabinet.*) Victor, don't.

VICTOR. (*Holds pose, but turns head for:*) Why not?

PARKER. (*With calm aplomb.*) Because our *liquor* supply is in there.

VICTOR. No more. We just killed the final quart.

GABY. (*Sardonically.*) "Oh churl, drunk all; and left no friendly drop to help me after?"

ROY. (*Uncowering from behind ladder.*) Isn't Juliet's tomb-speech a little sentimental for the occasion?

GABY. It's perfect. I was certain I'd find Victor dead of cirrhosis.

ROY. He hasn't licked out the bottles yet.

ALBERT. Then she still has a chance to follow after.

PARKER. Lie down, Albert.

ROY. Don't you do it, Albert. They can't keep you here against your will. Anytime you want to go, your clothes are in the bottom drawer of Victor's dresser.

VICTOR. *I* told Miss Hennebon to put them in the *closet.*

ROY. *My* things were in there!

GABY. Victor, if you're through playing with the tools, I'd like to start in on your wall.

VICTOR. (*Thrusts hammer and chisel at her.*) By all means! The damn thing was causing more nervous break-downs than a fire alarm in an oil refinery!

GABY. (*Grabbing tools from him.*) So *that's* what you think of my wedding present! *Now* the truth comes out! You never *did* like the mural—*or* the mobile!

VICTOR. I didn't say that. I liked them fine. It was most of my *patients* who did the complaining!

ALBERT. *I* think it's kind of *cute* . . .

PARKER. That's ten points for Victor.

GABY. I'll have you know a mural like that couldn't be purchased for less than ten thousand dollars!

VICTOR. You could've given me the *cash!*

GABY. I knew it! You *do* hate my mural! You always *did* hate it!

VICTOR. Now, Gaby—

GABY. You think it's disgusting and ugly and vile! I can read it in your face! I hate you!

ALBERT. If you hate him that much, why don't you *leave* it there? It'd serve him right.

VICTOR. Albert, lie down. (JINGLE—*dressed as before —enters from anteroom, carrying mixed sheaf of papers, some handwritten, some typewritten.*)

JINGLE. Victor, darling, I just *adore* your book! (*Waves sheets impatiently, trying to find the right expressive words.*) It's so true-to-life . . . so up-to-date . . . so *Now. . . !* But the ending— (*Sees* GABY, *smiles at her.*) Oh, hi! All recovered from your attack?

GABY. What attack?

VICTOR. Your fainting fits.

GABY. My what?

VICTOR. Well, she wanted to know who screamed, and why.

GABY. (*Having a fit:*) And *you* told *her* I had *fits?!*

VICTOR. Women who scream and faint when they feel like it must have *something!*

JINGLE. Oh, never mind about her, let's talk about your book. Why isn't it finished?

ALBERT. Because John Philip Sousa already *has* a wife.

VICTOR. (*To* JINGLE:) How could you have finished already? I didn't expect you back here for hours!

JINGLE. Well, I used to read really slow, but then one day I read this article on speed-reading in the Readers Digest—

VICTOR. (*Claps his right palm across his eyes.*) I'm losing my mind. I'm turning paranoid. I have this constant feeling that a national monthly magazine is out to *get* me!

GABY. Victor, I'm giving you one last chance. What, exactly, is your relationship with this woman?!

VICTOR. (*Uncovers eyes, extends hands pleadingly.*) Gaby—Gaby—you're simply going to have to *trust* me!

ROY. Don't listen to him, Gaby.

JINGLE. Victor, about the final chapter of your novel—

ROY. Novel? What's that about a *novel?!*

JINGLE. Well, Victor's written the most entertaining—

VICTOR. (*In desperation, embraces her.*) Don't listen to her! She's crazed with love! (*To* JINGLE:) Kiss me!

GABY. Victor!

VICTOR. (*To* GABY:) Trust me!

ALBERT. Can I have my Jingle now?

JINGLE. *Your* Jingle?

ALBERT. He promised.

GABY. Victor, *what* is going *on* here?! (CHARLOTTE *and* DOROTHEA, *in topcoats and hats, enter from anteroom;* CHARLOTTE *exits, with a wan smile and wave at* VICTOR, *into dressing room, on:*)

DOROTHEA. The fuzz confiscated my banner! They said it's state's evidence. (*Sees* ALBERT, *who has allowed blanket to slip to his waist.*) Albert, you go get your clothes on this minute!

ALBERT. Yes, Grandmother! (*Hops up, holding blanket about himself, and starts for balcony.*)

DOROTHEA. (*Removing topcoat.*) The idea, socializing with people in an outfit like that! (*Stands revealed in bathing suit, minus banner.*)

VICTOR. Albert, come back here, or I'll kiss Jingle—!

DOROTHEA. Albert, do as I say! (ALBERT, *who has nearly about-faced, exits up stairs into apartment at a clumsy trot.*)

ROY. I still want to know what Miss Jabonski meant about a novel!

GABY. You mean you haven't heard about Victor's novel?

PARKER. (*Lurches forward, grabs her shoulders so that*

she must face him.) Shut your pretty mouth and *kiss* me!

GABY. (*Struggling.*) Park, are you *crazy?!*

VICTOR. *Kiss* the man, darling!

GABY. But *Victor—!*

VICTOR. *Trust* me!

JINGLE. Victor, if you're not going through with our kiss, let go! My back is getting sweaty.

ROY. Mrs. Melnik, would you tell me what I'm being sued *for?*

GABY. (*Still shoulder-clasped by* PARKER.) Victor, *I* want to know what's going on with you and that woman!

ROY. (*To* GABY:) And what was that you started to say about Victor's *novel?* Why does *Albert* have to wind it up?

DOROTHEA. (*Brightening with pleasure.*) Do you mean *my* Albert is writing a novel?

VICTOR. Of course not!

JINGLE. Look, are you going to kiss me or aren't you?

VICTOR. Oh, what's the use! (*Releases her.*) Miss Jabonski, I'm sorry. The plain fact is, *I* don't love you, *Albert* does!

DOROTHEA. *My* Albert?

PARKER. But keeping the lovers apart is necessary to the treatment!

ROY. There *isn't* any such treatment! Victor, what has Albert *got?*

VICTOR. Ah-ah! Privileged communication!

ROY. You don't wriggle out of it *that* easily, Vic—! What sort of disease could a man have that makes it necessary to keep him away from the woman he loves—!? (*As others all stare accusingly at him:*) *I* don't mean *that* kind of disease! (ALBERT *enters from apartment, in shoes, socks, pants and shirt, his shirt collar open and no necktie, with his suit jacket over his arm.*)

ALBERT. Would somebody help me tie my shoes? (CHARLOTTE *enters from dressing room, in uniform, minus topcoat and hat, on:*)

JINGLE. Albert! (*Steps around* VICTOR, *the better to see him.*) Is it true what Victor said—do you really love me?

ROY. If Victor said it, I wouldn't believe a word of it!

GABY. (*Pulls free of* PARKER's *clasp.*) Now, just a minute, Roy—! Victor may be weak, and treacherous, and unreliable, but he is *not* a *liar!*

VICTOR. Thank you. I think.

ROY. Gaby, what do you *see* in that guy?

JINGLE. Will you all please stop interrupting?! Albert, answer the question!

ALBERT. (*Still on balcony, hesitantly.*) I can't.

DOROTHEA. For heaven's sake, why not, Albert?

ALBERT. Doctor Karleen said if I declared myself, it would ruin the cure.

ROY. *What* cure?

ALBERT. (*Fumbles envelope out of inner jacket pocket, clumsily, since jacket is still over his arm.*) Of my frustration. He says as soon as I reveal the final dream, I'll be sane again.

DOROTHEA. What do you mean, *"again?"*

VICTOR. (*Moves toward balcony.*) Albert, are you telling me the final dream's in that envelope?

PARKER. Impossible! When did he have time to write it *down?*

VICTOR. Even if he *found* the time, how can we end with John Philip Sousa!?

ALBERT. Oh, I made that part up. I didn't want to say anything in front of Doctor Terrigan. I mean, you and he are rival writers, and—

JINGLE. Albert! That's *reasonable!* You actually made a logical deduction!

VICTOR. You mean the stupid cure is *working?!*

CHARLOTTE. *I'd* like to say something . . .

GABY. (*As all heads turn toward* CHARLOTTE:) *What* would you like to say?

CHARLOTTE. *Anything.* I just felt left out.

PARKER. Look, things are tough enough already with the *rest* of us talking!

JINGLE. All *I* want to hear is *Albert!* Do you love me or don't you!?

ROY. First things first! *I* want to see what's in that *envelope!* (*Starts across room toward* ALBERT.)

GABY. I don't understand—does his dream have something to do with Victor's novel, or what?

VICTOR. Stop saying *"novel"!* (*Grabs* ROY'S *shoulders from behind.*) Now, hold on a moment, Roy . . . there are some doctor-patient secrets that shouldn't be—

ROY. (*Pulls free, starts run toward foot of stairs.*) The hell with ethics! I want a look in that envelope!

ALBERT. (*Clambering over railing.*) No, please, it's very personal—! (*Jumps onto desktop, loses balance, falls backward toward right, where* PARKER *and* CHAR-LOTTE *and* JINGLE *will catch him, on:*) Yaaaaaaa!

DOROTHEA. Albert, you mustn't put your feet on the furniture.

CHARLOTTE. (*Who is nearest his head as they lower him to floor.*) Albert, are you all right?

ALBERT. (*Flinging an arm around her neck.*) I am *now!* As long as *you're* near me, everything's all right!

ROY. (*Who had been stymied on stairs, heads back down and around desk, on:*) Are you crazy? That's Charlotte!

CHARLOTTE. Doctor Terrigan, I've been a nurse for twenty-seven years, and a spinster for more than fifty. Majority rules. Shut up, Doc!

JINGLE. Doctor Karleen, you said Albert was in love with *me!*

VICTOR. I can't be right *all* the time! . . . Not even *some* of the time.

ROY. (*Till now semi-impeded by* PARKER *and* JINGLE, *suddenly grabs envelope from* ALBERT.) Got it! (*Runs with it as* VICTOR *takes after him, the two men circling prostrate* ALBERT; PARKER *and* JINGLE *and* CHARLOTTE *still at their assorted catching-*ALBERT *position about the* *body, on:*) *Now* we'll find out the solution to all this craziness!

VICTOR. Roy, wait— Listen— You don't understand—

GABY. Will somebody please tell me what's going on here?!

DOROTHEA. Dear, it's about time you learned the facts of life: All psychiatrists are nuts. (ROY *has made it to chaise, leaped upon it, and now stands fending off attempted similar leaps by* VICTOR, *pushing him back to floor level with one hand, while holding envelope aloft in other.*)

VICTOR. Give me that, before I call the police!

PARKER. Victor, no! You *can't* call the police, remember!? Think of the publicity—your career—!

VICTOR. You've got as big a stake in this as I have! Help me! Or I'll say you were my accomplice!

PARKER. (*Piously.*) I haven't the faintest idea what you're talking about!

CHARLOTTE. (*Helping* ALBERT *to his feet.*) Albert, I had no idea you cared for me . . .

ALBERT. From the first day I saw you, in here. That's probably why you showed up as the secret identity of the masked rider. (PARKER *and* VICTOR *gasp, both turning from* ROY, *who will tear open envelope during:*)

PARKER. Don't listen to him!

VICTOR. He's crazy! A raving lunatic! A certifiable maniac!

DOROTHEA. I'm so proud . . . !

ROY. (*Reads folded paper inside envelope; it only takes a second to read; then he shrieks:*) *Oh, noooooo—!*

JINGLE. (*Galvanized.*) Good grief, Doctor Terrigan, what *is* it?!

ROY. A *subpoena!* (ALBERT *smiles with surprising shrewdness.*)

VICTOR. (*Realizes, whirls to face* ALBERT.) You! You're the process-server?!

PARKER. But I thought the process-server was the doorman's brother!

DOROTHEA. Don't see why he *can't* be . . . *I'm* the doorman's *grandmother* . . . !

VICTOR. But Roy—I thought you already figured out Mrs. Melnik doesn't have a case—?!

DOROTHEA. Oh, *I'm* not suing him.

GABY. Then who *is?*

ALBERT. His wife, for desertion and non-support.

GABY. *Wife?* Roy, you have a *wife?*

ROY. Now, now, Gaby—

GABY. And to think I *swallowed* all that romantic jazz you were handing me in Victor's apartment—! (*Realizes what she has said, stops guiltily and turns to flash sickly smile at* VICTOR.) Uh—that is—not *ro-man-tic* exactly . . .

VICTOR. In my own *apartment?* Have you no shame?!

GABY. It didn't start out like that, honestly it didn't. I was trying to figure out your mental state, and Roy made us a couple of drinks, and—well—your sofa was kind of comfy, and—

VICTOR. And you had the nerve to come out on the balcony, right after dallying with the enemy, and *scream* at *me*—?!

GABY. At the time, it seemed like a clever cover-up . . . Oh, Victor, what can I say?

PARKER. Wait a minute, wait a minute, everybody! Let me get this straight . . . Albert isn't really a mental case?

ALBERT. No, I made that up to get into Doctor Karleen's office.

VICTOR. So Mrs. Melnik isn't really a mental case, either?

DOROTHEA. Oh, yes. *I* am!

PARKER. But what about Albert's dreams? What about Lady Jessica and Sir Frederick, and how she finds true love at last?

ALBERT. Gee, I'm sorry, I have no idea of the outcome. I usually get the subpoena *served* before I get *this* far in a book.

VICTOR. You mean you've pulled this dream-novel stunt *before?*

DOROTHEA. Albert's *specialty* is *psychiatrists.* He serves them all the time.

ALBERT. You'd be surprised how many of them have unhappy love-lives.

VICTOR. No I wouldn't.

JINGLE. Then you don't really love me? You only pretended to love me so Doctor Karleen would get scared and keep you prisoner here so you could be here when Doctor Terrigan showed up to hide?

ALBERT. I suppose you hate me for deceiving you.

JINGLE. No, actually, I'm relieved. I mean, who wants to think she's the best beloved of a mental case?

ROY. (*Who by now has sat down sadly on chaise, staring unhappily at subpoena.*) Then why did you keep behaving as though you loved him back?

JINGLE. I was just trying to be neighborly . . .

ROY. (*Suddenly wide-eyed, jumps to his feet.*) Parker—! I just realized—! If the lawsuit's not about the book—!

PARKER. (*Suddenly gleeful, rushes to him.*) We can get it back on the shelves! We'll make the Christmas lists after all!

ROY. (*As he and* PARKER *start happily toward door.*) And I can use the royalties to get myself a really good lawyer—!

PARKER. Hell, even if you *lose* your case, you'll be able to afford the damages your wife is asking—! (*At brink of anteroom, turns to look at* VICTOR.) Uh . . . I don't suppose there's any chance you *might* figure out a finale to that novel—?

VICTOR. Park! You mean—you'd still *publish* it?

PARKER. Well, casebooks come and casebooks go, but sex is here to stay! (*Exits with* ROY.)

GABY. Victor, I don't understand any of this. That book you were writing—

ALBERT. Listen, I hate to dash your hopes, Doctor, but

that plot is the property of the District Attorney's office, since I'm the author.

CHARLOTTE. Oh, but Albert—you wouldn't mind giving it to Doctor Karleen, would you? After all, *my* name's in it, right? And you wouldn't want your sweetheart's name bandied about in criminal court?

DOROTHEA. Oh, let him *have* the book, Albert. You can always write another.

ALBERT. But I need it for my job!

CHARLOTTE. No, you don't. I'll support the two of us. (*Looks at* VICTOR.) Of course, my present salary—

VICTOR. —has just been doubled!

ALBERT. Wow! This is really terrific of you, Miss Hennebon— Oh, I guess I can call you "Charlotte," now, huh?

DOROTHEA. (*Who has gotten her coat and hat, by now.*) Maybe even "Masked Rider"! Lovers should always have pet names. (*Exits to anteroom.*)

CHARLOTTE. (*Moving same direction, arm-in-arm with* ALBERT:) Why *did* you choose me to the masked rider, Albert? I mean, you could have made me one of the gypsies, or the girl who has the triplets, or even Lady Jessica's maid . . .

ALBERT. Because from the first moment I looked at your face, something deep inside of me said, "Gee, she'd look *so* great with a *mask* on!" (CHARLOTTE *reacts, but when you're a fiftyish spinster you can't be choosy, so she links her arm even more snugly in his, sighs, and the two of them exit through anteroom doorway.*)

GABY. (*To* VICTOR, *quietly.*) Well, where do we go from here?

VICTOR. (*Gently.*) *You* go upstairs and freshen up. Then come back down here and I'm taking you out to dinner. *You* can pick up the check.

GABY. I don't deserve you.

VICTOR. I don't deserve you, either. But God bless our dumb luck! (GABY *smiles, very happy, then hurries up stairs and through door to apartment, leaving it ajar;*

JINGLE, *who has been standing watching all this, now extends her hand to shake* VICTOR'S.)

JINGLE. Well, you're the second lover I've lost, today. But thanks for a couple of lovely memories, Doc.

VICTOR. (*Retaining her hand after the shake.*) I was pretty rotten to you, wasn't I! All that wild kissing, just to keep a hold on Albert . . . (*Chuckles ruefully.*) I just realized—without Albert, the rest of the book won't do me a bit of good, anyhow. I can't plot worth a damn.

JINGLE. I wish you *had* written the book. It was pretty terrific. I was so *sure* it had been written by you . . .

VICTOR. Really? What made you think that?

JINGLE. Well . . . when you kissed me . . . aw, you don't want to hear this . . .

VICTOR. Please. I'm really interested. *Why* did you think it was mine?

JINGLE. (*Almost blushing, and suddenly shy.*) Because—well—I don't go having wild sexy daydreams, as a usual thing—but somehow—when you were kissing me —well, I had some notions that would make Lady Jessica blush!

VICTOR. About me, you mean?

JINGLE. You? Oh, gosh, no! Oh, gee, I didn't mean anything like *that!*

VICTOR. Then—about who?

JINGLE. Lady Jessica, of course. The whole book was kind of spinning around in my head, and when your lips touched mine—things began to happen—to the characters.

VICTOR. You mean—just because I kissed you—and you thought the book was mine—you actually started seeing re-runs of the plot?

JINGLE. No, not re-runs— Brand-*new* stuff. Crazy, huh?

VICTOR. (*Gently reaches out, pulls her to him, during:*) I'm a psychiatrist. I *like* crazy things. I wonder—strictly in the interests of psychiatric science—if we might try a little experiment . . . ?

JINGLE. (*Watching his arms go around her, warily.*) What *kind* of experiment? I mean, I'm neighborly as the next girl but— (*He kisses her; she kisses back; then she leans her face back from his, and says:*) Wowee! Is that ever *wild!* Lady Jessica just got shanghaied on a whaler out of New Bedford. She's the only woman among seventy love-crazed sailors. Can you *imagine* that?

VICTOR. If I could imagine *that*, I wouldn't be doing *this!* (*Kisses her again.*)

JINGLE. (*Pulls back face as before, and:*) *Criminy!* The first mate fell in love with her, and he's just challenged the entire crew to a duel with harpoon-guns!

VICTOR. I'll never remember all this. Quick, where's my tape recorder?

JINGLE. Hey, *I* can take shorthand—!

VICTOR. Then what are we waiting for! (*Half-drags her to desk, pulls her down on his lap, thrusts notepad and pencil into her hands, gets a friendly embrace around her, and:*) Now, let's get to work. You concentrate on love, and I'll concentrate on that Pulitzer Prize . . . ! (*Kisses her again, but good, as a freshened-up* GABY *steps out on balcony, gapes down at them for a split second, then cries:*)

GABY. Victor! Why are you kissing that woman!?

VICTOR. Do you want a honeymoon on *Bear Mountain?!*

GABY. Instead of the Caribbean? Of course not!

VICTOR. Then for heaven's sake, darling, *trust* me! (*And as he fervently kisses a compliant* JINGLE *again, and* GABY *gapes and gasps and tries to think what to scream at him—*)

THE CURTAIN FALLS

PROPERTIES

ACT ONE

Preset:
  notepad and pen/pencil cannister on desk
  paint-spattered canvas dropcloth on chaise
  small stepladder
  lots of glasses, bottles of liquor, in phonograph/liquor cabinet
    with medium supply of ice cubes also available inside. it

Worn or carried on by:
  ROY: pipe in mouth at first entrance (optional)

  CHARLOTTE: overcoat and hat, nurse's cap

  PARKER: typewritten manuscript, topcoat, checkbook, pen

  ALBERT: two bundles of handwritten sheets of manuscript,
    one large, one small, inside jacket pocket, $25 in bills

  VICTOR: wristwatch, overcoat

  GABY: hat, fur stole

ACT TWO

Preset:
  Icebag on Victor's face

Worn or carried on by:

  DOROTHEA: long black coat, hat, purse containing more hand-
    written manuscript sheets, banner reading "MISS OCTO-
    BER 1929"

  CHARLOTTE: stethoscope, Albert's bundled clothing and shoes

  ROY: homburg, overcoat, suitcase, glass of hangover remedy,
    smoking jacket with complementary scarf

  GABY: engagement ring

  ALBERT: topcoat, copy of Readers Digest

  DOROTHEA: copy of Readers Digest, coat, hat, purse

ACT THREE

Preset:
stepladder
mobile in wastebasket, visible
cigarette butts in floorstand ashtray
lighted cigarette in Victor's hand
blanket around Albert
Victor's and Parker's suit jacket and ties on coat tree
Note pad and pen/pencil cannister on desk

Worn or carried on by:
ROY: homburg, overcoat, suitcase

GABY: hammer and chisel

JINGLE: sheaf of mixed typewritten/handwritten manuscript
pages

CHARLOTTE and DOROTHEA: topcoats and hats

ALBERT: suit jacket over arm with envelope in inner pocket
with subpoena in envelope

SOUND EFFECTS

ACT ONE

pre-taped recording of "Brahms Lullaby"—about three minutes
   long
telephone bell
rap at door to anteroom
slam of outer office door

ACT TWO

pre-taped recording of Ravel's "Pavane pour Une Enfante Defunte"
telephone bell
police siren—clear but far below apparent window-height by
   soft sound of it
pre-taped recording of love-theme portion of Tchaikovsky's
   "Romeo and Juliet Overture"

ACT THREE

pre-taped recording of Sousa's "Stars and Stripes Forever"

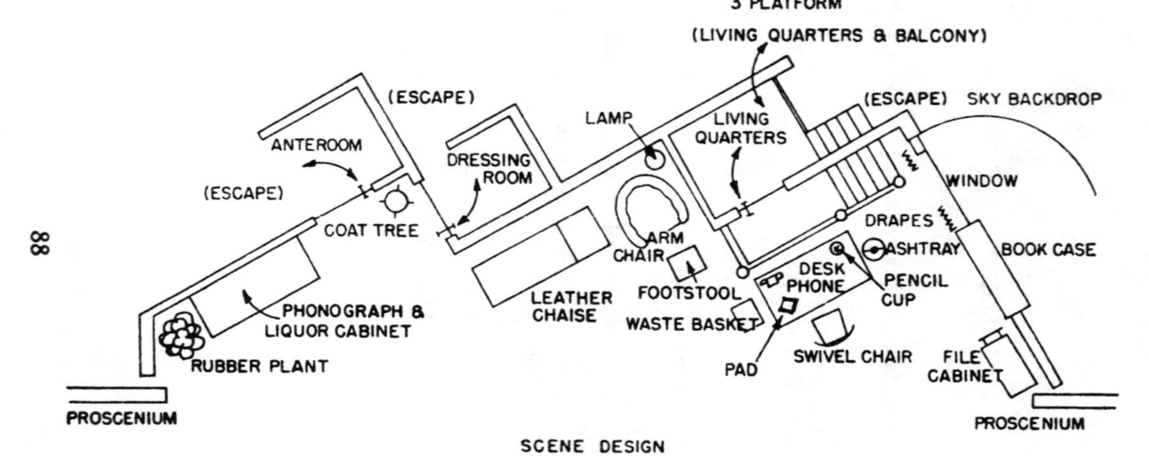

SCENE DESIGN
"MEANWHILE, BACK ON THE COUCH..."

For all enquiries regarding motion picture, television, and other media rights, please contact Samuel French.

MUSIC USE NOTE

Licensees are solely responsible for obtaining formal written permission from copyright owners to use copyrighted music in the performance of this play and are strongly cautioned to do so. If no such permission is obtained by the licensee, then the licensee must use only original music that the licensee owns and controls. Licensees are solely responsible and liable for all music clearances and shall indemnify the copyright owners of the play(s) and their licensing agent, Samuel French, against any costs, expenses, losses and liabilities arising from the use of music by licensees. Please contact the appropriate music licensing authority in your territory for the rights to any incidental music.

IMPORTANT BILLING AND CREDIT REQUIREMENTS

If you have obtained performance rights to this title, please refer to your licensing agreement for important billing and credit requirements.